P9-ARJ-347

DISCOVER AN [illegible] MYSTERY SERIES, MEET A FEISTY FEMALE SLEUTH, AND ENJOY AN AWARD-WINNING AUTHOR—

SHERRYL WOODS

❖❖❖

"Woods has an excellent ear for dialogue and an unerring sense of pacing."

—***Publishers Weekly***

❖

"Amanda's got guts, good instincts, and a brave heart. From now on, she's definitely high on my reading list. Woods is a terrific writer . . . fresh, fast-paced, original."

—**Carolyn G. Hart, Agatha and Anthony Award-winning author of *Southern Ghost***

❖

"Ms. Woods has really hit upon a winning ticket with the feisty Amanda." —***Rave Reviews***

❖

"Energetic, outspoken. . . . Amanda goes after her story like a dog who has latched onto a dirty sock for life."

—***Mystery Scene***

❖

"Particularly wonderful is the mix of Southerners invaded by some Northern folks . . . realistic characters are captivating while she advances us through a suspenseful, sometimes humorous, whodunit."

—***Mystery News* on *Ties That Bind***

ALSO BY SHERRYL WOODS

Published by
WARNER BOOKS

ATTENTION: SCHOOLS AND CORPORATIONS

WARNER books are available at quantity discounts with bulk purchase for educational, business, or sales promotional use. For information, please write to: SPECIAL SALES DEPARTMENT, WARNER BOOKS, 1271 AVENUE OF THE AMERICAS, NEW YORK, N.Y. 10020

ARE THERE WARNER BOOKS
YOU WANT BUT CANNOT FIND IN YOUR LOCAL STORES?

You can get any WARNER BOOKS title in print. Simply send title and retail price, plus 95¢ per order and 95¢ per copy to cover mailing and handling costs for each book desired. New York State and California residents add applicable sales tax. Enclose check or money order only, no cash please, to: WARNER BOOKS, P.O. BOX 690, NEW YORK, N.Y. 10019

Sherryl Woods

Body and Soul

A Time Warner Company

If you purchase this book without a cover you should be aware that this book may have been stolen property and reported as "unsold and destroyed" to the publisher. In such case neither the author nor the publisher has received any payment for this "stripped book."

WARNER BOOKS EDITION

Copyright © 1989 by Sherryl Woods
All rights reserved.

Cover design by Jackie Merri Meyer
Cover photo by Herman Estevez
Hand lettering by Carl Dellacroce

Warner Books, Inc.
1271 Avenue of the Americas
New York, NY 10020

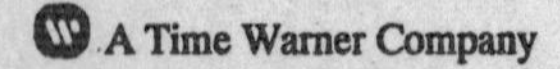

Printed in the United States of America

First Printing: August, 1989

Reissued: July, 1994

10 9 8 7 6 5 4 3 2

CHAPTER
One

Amanda gasped for breath. Her side ached. There were shooting pains in her legs. She bent over, ready to plead for mercy if it would end the unrelenting, painful torture. She no longer cared about salvaging her pride. She wanted to survive. Five more minutes and they'd have to call in the paramedics to revive her. She closed her eyes and tried not to think about how much it hurt. But a sadistically cheerful voice continued to torment her with its cruel demands.

"Lift those knees. Higher! Get 'em up, Amanda. Don't you dare stop now. You too, Jolene, Mary Beth. Lift 'em. Nineteen, twenty. Lift and kick. Lift and kick. Come on, ladies and gentlemen. This ain't no Sunday afternoon stroll. Twenty-three, twenty-four. Keep going now. No pain, no gain."

By the count of thirty-seven, Amanda's thigh muscles were protesting even more emphatically. By forty-one, her knees had turned to jelly. And this was only the end of the warm-up routine! She glared at the aerobics instructor, then at Jenny Lee Macon, who'd talked her into joining this class two weeks ago. Neither one of them was even breathing hard. Reaching the count of fifty once again became a matter of honor.

Of course, she consoled herself when her lungs and legs gave out at forty-seven, Jenny Lee was twenty-two years old and weighed no more than 105 pounds soaking wet and fully clothed. She had no more need for an aerobics class than the instructor, Carrie Owens, who looked as though she existed on alfalfa sprouts.

Personally, Amanda thought there was probably something unhealthy—if not un-American—about a twenty-inch waistline and shapely legs that displayed not the first hint of cellulite. It was especially disgusting on a woman whose face evidenced a certain maturity. Amanda guessed that Carrie Owens was approaching forty years of age. Amanda was a decade younger, which made her state of near collapse all the harder to take.

These classes had merely confirmed her oft-stated opinion that health clubs had been created by descendants of the Marquis de Sade and that the instructors were his personal representatives. She didn't care that the club, Weights and Measures, was decorated in soothing tones of gray and mauve. Nor was she fooled by the classical music that was piped in whenever aerobics classes weren't in session. The place was a den of torture. All those elaborate machines told the story. The resemblance to some well-equipped ancient dungeon was unmistakable.

Jenny Lee, however, had suggested that there might be a story here for their employer, *Inside Atlanta* magazine, a look at how health clubs had become the singles bars of the eighties. As a reporter always in search of a solid feature, Amanda had been tempted enough to overcome all of her instinctive wariness.

The hour-long, intricately choreographed aerobics session continued. As she panted through scattered parts of it, Amanda wondered why someone with Carrie's ingenuity wasn't doing Broadway musicals. She decided it was entirely likely that no chorus line could keep up with her.

Finally, the taped music ground to a halt. Some of the participants actually had enough breath to cheer. Amanda settled for casting a longing glance in the direction of the steam room and showers.

"Oh, no, you don't," Jenny Lee said, tugging her toward the weights. The girl's artfully highlighted brown hair wasn't even mussed, Amanda noted. Then she caught a glimpse of her own straggly locks in one of the wall-to-ceiling mirrors designed to remind members why they were there.

"You haven't done the whole routine," Jenny Lee said with what Amanda interpreted as uncalled-for glee.

The whole routine. The words loomed as ominously as images of the rack in another age. "I am only here to do research, not to die in the attempt," Amanda protested weakly.

"As long as the magazine's paying for your thirty-day introductory membership, you might as well take advantage of it."

"I just hope my insurance is paid up," Amanda muttered darkly.

Jenny Lee grinned and gave her a maternal pat, which was somewhat inappropriate since Amanda was nearly seven years older than her friend.

"Medical or life?" Jenny Lee inquired.

Amanda moaned as her calf muscle cramped. "Both."

"I'll check the personnel records tomorrow," she promised.

Amanda's scowl deepened. With a final baleful glance, she limped off to one of the weight machines. She selected the one that merely required her to tug on a pulley and lift what felt like a four-hundred-pound weight with arms that already felt like lead. Three machines and twenty minutes of agony later Jenny Lee came over to confide that she'd met the nicest man over by the rowing machine.

"See the tall guy with brown hair and glasses? Isn't he the cutest thing? He's invited me out for dinner, but I have time if you want to spend a few minutes in the steam room," she said with so much energy and cheerfulness that Amanda seriously considered dropping a five-pound weight on her toes.

"You go on. I want to be left alone to die," Amanda moaned, swiping strands of damp blond hair out of her face.

For the first time all night, Jenny Lee looked contrite. "Oh, you poor baby. You really are a little sore, aren't you?"

Amanda's eyebrows rose at the understatement.

"Come on," Jenny Lee insisted. "The steam will help."

"Twelve weeks with a masseur wouldn't help."

Just then a woman's scream punctuated Beethoven's Ninth Symphony. It rose above the hum of conversation and the metallic clank of weights. From its bloodcurdling tone Amanda doubted the cry was a reaction to a weight loss. Near silence fell throughout the club and all movement stopped. Only the symphony played on. Everyone stared in the direction of the women's locker room.

Amanda was the first to react. Cursing her muscles which were solidifying into knots, she hobbled into the locker room, where women in various stages of undress were frozen by shock and uncertainty. As she came to the steam room, she bumped into a shaking, terrified woman who was backing out of the door followed by puffs of steam. It created an eerie effect.

Amanda put a consoling arm around the woman's shoulders. "What is it?" she asked in a deliberately quiet, soothing voice. "Are you okay?"

Clutching a towel around herself with one white-knuckled hand, the woman stared back at Amanda with wide, unseeing eyes. Finally, still shaking, she pointed inside. Her mouth opened and closed, but no words came out.

Taking a deep breath, Amanda stepped forward into the steam. It rose up around her in an enveloping wave of heat permeated by the lingering odor of sweat and a hint of the sauna's eucalyptus scent. The visibility was worse than a Georgia country road during a twilight gullywasher. It didn't help that she had no idea where to look to find whatever had frightened the woman into that chilling scream.

As if to confirm her suspicion, she immediately tripped over something large and solid, something that she sensed had no business being on the floor. Her heart lurched unsteadily as she stooped down and came face to face with the aerobics instructor, who appeared from her vacant stare and blue tinged lips to be very, very dead. Amanda swallowed hard and felt for a pulse. Her own was racing, but the instructor's was nonexistent.

"Somebody call 911," she called through the door, then added as an afterthought, "and turn off this damn steam."

There was a slight hiss of sound and the room began to clear and cool. For the first time, Amanda could see Carrie Owens clearly. There were no visible bruises, no scratches, no signs of a struggle. Still, a woman who lived on health food did not generally die of natural causes in her late thirties—unless perhaps she'd starved to death. Amanda's heartbeat quickened and this time it had nothing to do with exertion. The prospect of a good story always excited her.

For the moment, though, the story had to wait. Policemen and paramedics descended amidst wailing sirens. Detective Jim Harrison, Homicide, arrived more sedately. He looked rumpled and tired, as though he'd been on duty for two days straight and hadn't seen anything very pretty in all that time. He made Columbo look chic.

After convincing himself that Carrie was, indeed, dead, he commandeered an office. He waved at Amanda to follow.

"So," he said after she'd identified herself and told him she was a reporter, "you're the one who found the body."

"No. Actually, that was one of the other members. She screamed. When I got to the steam room, she was coming out."

"How did she seem?"

Amanda thought it an odd question. "I don't understand."

"Miss Roberts, you just told me you're a reporter. You're trained to observe people. What was your impression of this woman you say had just discovered a body?"

"She was terrified."

"Not guilty?"

An interesting idea. Amanda considered it, then dismissed it. "I don't think so. Unless she's really cold-blooded and a consummate actress, I doubt she could have pulled it off. The woman who screamed sounded and looked genuinely frightened."

The questioning went on a few more minutes before Detective Harrison released her. "Stop by the station later to give a formal statement."

Amanda nodded.

"Oh, *Ms*. Roberts," he said, halting her flight back to her notebook. "Are you planning on writing about this?"

"I have to discuss that with my editor." She considered it a fairly adept evasion. Policemen tended to get nervous when reporters were first on the scene of anything.

"If you run across anything you think I should know, you will let me know, won't you?"

He actually made it sound like a respectful request,

rather than a command from General Patton. She found herself responding with a smile and a nod of assent. At the time she meant it.

She went back to the locker room, which was still crowded and hushed. Unable to take a shower without an audience that included several crime scene experts from the Atlanta PD, she sponged off as best she could and changed into a blouse and slacks. Grabbing her purse, she dug out her notebook and a handful of assorted jelly beans. She intentionally selected the fruit flavors as a concession to her fitness-oriented surroundings, then wondered why she'd bothered. The atmosphere hadn't done anything for poor Carrie's health.

As the police conducted their investigation, she began her own, starting with the woman who'd discovered the body. She found out her name from Jenny Lee—Felicia Grant. She was sitting in front of her locker, still wrapped in a towel, still looking dazed. Apparently Detective Harrison was saving her for last. Amanda sat down beside her.

Felicia Grant was one of those fortunate women whose ages are impossible to pin down simply by appearance. Her complexion was flawless, her hair a stunning shade of auburn that could have been natural, her figure unblemished by a single ounce of extra fat. She could have been twenty-eight or thirty-eight or anything in between. But the hint of weariness in her startling blue-green eyes made Amanda think she was probably closer to thirty-eight.

"Did you see Carrie go into the steam room?" she asked after introducing herself.

Felicia stared at her as if she'd just realized Amanda was there. She shook her head.

"Did you see anyone come out of the steam room?"

The question hung in the air for a tense interval before finally sinking in. Felicia's eyes widened and all the color drained from her face. "You think she was murdered, don't you?" she said in a breathless, horrified whisper. "Oh my God, what if the murderer thinks I'm a witness?" Her fingers clamped around Amanda's wrist.

"Are you?" she said, trying to loosen Felicia's hold by gently patting her hand. She finally let go and Amanda rubbed the marks left on her wrist.

"No. I mean I don't remember. I don't think so." Felicia buried her face in her hands. "Oh, this is just so awful. Who would do something like this to Carrie? Couldn't it have been a heart attack or something?"

There was a pleading note in her voice. It was not the tone of a woman who already knew better. Once more Amanda dismissed Detective Harrison's theory that Felicia might have been responsible for Carrie's death.

"It's possible she died of natural causes," Amanda said, though she had no intention of waiting for an official determination before asking her questions. Now, with everyone's guard down, was the time to get totally honest, uncensored answers. "How well did you know Carrie?"

"Not well at all. I usually take aerobics in the morning. Today I had a scheduling conflict. I decided to come tonight. I don't like to miss a day. Other than tonight I've only seen her when she's substituted a couple of times with the morning class. Everyone thinks she's tough, but terrific."

Suddenly she regarded Amanda curiously. "Why are you asking all this? You're not with the police, are you?"

"No. I explained that before. I'm a reporter with *Inside Atlanta*."

This time it apparently sank in. Felicia became even edgier. "I don't want my name mixed up in this. If you're going to write something, leave me out of it."

"I can't promise to do that."

"Please, you have to promise me you won't use my name. What if she was murdered? The killer could come looking for me."

Amanda saw no point in reminding her that in all likelihood the killer already knew perfectly well who had discovered the body. Before she could reply, a man dressed in chic gray slacks broke through the crowd and came to Felicia's side. She fell into his arms, sobbing. Amanda stuck around just long enough to determine that the man was her fiancé. That led her to take a closer look at the diamond on Felicia's ring finger. Her conclusive impression was one of wealth, country-club wealth. It was interesting that the two of them would be in a modest little fitness club such as this.

She left them and went in search of Robert Barnes, one of the two owners of Weights and Measures. He was the only one she'd seen around that night. The other owner, Jackson Greybar, was generally elusive. She'd just spotted Robert, when a shadow loomed over her.

"I should have known," Joe Donelli said, his voice

laced with Brooklyn-accented exasperation, his expression long suffering.

Donelli was an ex-cop-turned-farmer with whom she shared a certain intellectual rapport and enough electricity to light downtown Atlanta. However, despite the very positive aspects of the fairly new relationship, they were still working on the details. Some of them weren't going to be so easy to resolve.

For one thing, he did not exactly approve of her career as an investigative reporter for *Inside Atlanta*, any more than he had liked it when she was working for a rural weekly and chasing a famous chef's murderer at the time they'd met. He tolerated her chosen career for her sake, but he'd made it clear on more than one occasion that he would prefer it if she took up knitting instead. Tonight seemed to be one of those occasions.

Actually, she supposed it was not her occupation Donelli objected to so much as the way she went about it. She tended to plunge into the middle of things regardless of the danger. It made for great copy, but it had also resulted in a few hair-raising incidents, not the least of which had been having her car bombed in New York and being shot at a few months earlier right there in Georgia.

Unfortunately she had shared the details of those mishaps before realizing that Donelli was by nature protective. Since then she'd vowed to minimize the risks she undertook. His arrival to pick her up for dinner couldn't have been more poorly timed. Any dimwit could see that this latest story of hers had gone from inconsequential fluff to potential danger. Donelli was far from dim. He was scowling down at her now. He looked very much like a man intent on whisking her through the nearest exit. She dug in her heels in preparation. Donelli might possess a chunk of her heart, but he'd never control her actions. Intellectually he understood that. But it still grated on his macho streak.

"Can't you go anywhere without getting into trouble?" he asked. Despite the attempt at lightness, there was no mistaking the familiar air of resignation in his voice.

Amanda grinned. It was almost comforting to realize that some things about Donelli would never change. She assumed her most innocent expression. "Hey, I'm not the one who killed her."

Jenny Lee arrived just in time to overhear the gist of the conversation. "She's not," she confirmed helpfully. "I was with her the whole time."

"Thank you very much," Amanda said, giving Donelli a smug smile. "Ask the police. I've already told them everything I know. I wasn't even the one who discovered the body."

"Then, if you've already given your statement, you're probably free to leave," he said. "I've made a reservation."

"But—"

"Amanda!"

She lowered her voice to an emphatic hiss. "Didn't you hear me? Carrie Owens might have been murdered. I can't just leave now."

"You can." His brown-eyed gaze challenged her. Her chin tilted stubbornly. Finally, he sighed. "But you won't.

Okay, go on and do your thing. I'll wait. I'll even call the restaurant. Just one question, though."

Amanda waited.

"Isn't it a little pointless to cover a possible murder for a magazine that won't be out for another six weeks? People will have forgotten all about it by the time *Inside Atlanta* hits the newsstands."

"Not if this turns out to be some complicated case that the police can't solve overnight. Besides, I'll be able to do the sort of in-depth feature on Carrie and what happened to her that the newspapers don't have time to do. Maybe it won't even be a story, I mean if she just died or something, but I won't know that until we get the cause of death. Meantime, I think I ought to dig into it, you know, just in case."

She wound down finally and stared at him hopefully. She had no intention of leaving, but it would be nice if he understood. Donelli shook his head and waved her away. "Go. Dig. Enjoy."

Amanda started to look for Robert Barnes again, then turned back. "Why don't you talk to the police?" she suggested casually, avoiding Donelli's gaze. "See what they've found out."

Her comment drew another, more ferocious scowl. "Don't start, Amanda. I don't want to know what they found out."

"Of course, you do."

"No. Unlike you, I'd be perfectly content to walk out of here and leave the police to do their job."

It was an ongoing battle. She thought Donelli missed

police work. He claimed he actually liked raising tomatoes and lettuce and fighting insects instead of crime. Amanda studied his implacable expression and decided that it was not the time for another skirmish. She'd scatter clues for him later, knowing full well that he would be unable to resist trying to piece them together.

Over the next hour Amanda talked with almost everyone who had been in the aerobics class, as well as the employees of Weights and Measures. Since the naïve among them were still convinced that Carrie had keeled over from some undiscovered heart ailment, Amanda kept her questions focused on the woman herself.

She discovered that Carrie had been with the health club for six months, that she was dating one of the male instructors who happened to be off duty tonight, and that she was a very popular lady. Her classes were always filled to capacity with men and women who swore they'd never felt healthier—all because of her.

"Were you here when it happened?" she asked Robert Barnes, when she found him again. He was ashen beneath his carefully cultivated tan. Robert appeared to take full advantage of the club's equipment. He was lean and muscular, a fact he displayed to advantage by wearing shorts and tank tops most of the time. Tonight, apparently in honor of the solemnity of the situation, he was wearing jeans and an Izod shirt.

"No. I'd left for the evening. One of the men called me at home. I'd just started cooking dinner." He sank down on one of the locker room benches. "I can't believe it. I'd talked to her right before I left. She had all these plans for a new aerobics routine, something for the advanced students. She thought they were getting bored with the easy stuff."

Amanda blinked. *Easy stuff?* No doubt only Marine Corps recruits and professional athletes would qualify for Carrie's notion of advanced aerobics.

"As far as you knew she was feeling okay?"

"Okay? The woman had more energy than the rest of the staff combined," he said with a certain amount of awe. Amanda could readily identify with his attitude. "She was the ideal instructor."

"Where'd she come from?"

"I don't remember. I'd have to check her file. I think she'd been with another club here in town for a year or so and before that she lived someplace out of state."

"How did she get along with the other instructors? Any jealousy?"

Without hesitation he shook his head. "None I knew about."

"Did you hire her or did your partner?"

"We both approved her hiring. That's the way we run the place." His tone had a trace of defensiveness. "What are you trying to get at?"

"Nothing specific. I was just wondering." She smiled. "You know how reporters can't resist asking questions."

"Well, watch your implications. She was a good lady. I'd hate to see a hatchet job done on her when she can't defend herself. Know what I mean?"

Amanda nodded. Apparently satisfied with her intentions, Robert walked away. After he'd gone, she wondered how on earth anyone could do a hatchet job on a woman as terrific as the Carrie Owens he had just described. If he'd wanted to arouse her curiosity, he couldn't have done it more effectively.

For the moment, though, Amanda thought she'd done about as much as she could. The police were wrapping things up and most of the crowd had been sent home after giving preliminary statements. She went hunting for Donelli. She found him chatting with the policeman guarding the front door. She noticed he was careful not to introduce her as he led her away from the health club.

"What were you talking to him about?"

"The Falcons."

She regarded him skeptically. "With a dead woman not fifty yards away, you were discussing football?"

"We talked about the Braves first."

"Donelli!"

"What? You sound as though you think we were being sacrilegious or something. We didn't even know her."

"Don't get cute with me, Donelli. Didn't you even ask him what the police suspect happened?"

Donelli began whistling. He affected a look of such innocence that Amanda knew he was feeling guilty as hell. She grabbed his arm, planted her feet and waited until he jerked to a halt.

"You did ask him, didn't you?"

"I asked."

"And?"

"They seem to think she might have been smothered with the towel they found lying next to her."

"I knew it!" she exclaimed triumphantly.

"Amanda, will you stop gloating? What difference does it make? This will be a three-inch item buried on an inside page of the morning paper. Despite your hopes, it is not the beginning of some exposé."

"Donelli, this is not Brooklyn. People there may take murder in stride, but down here it's still news. A popular fitness instructor is dead, very likely murdered. And in a steam room yet."

"It has all the makings of one of those splashy tabloid headlines," he agreed, knowing it would irritate her. Amanda considered her work serious, well-researched investigative journalism. She despised sensational pulp.

"Aren't you the least bit curious about what happened and why?"

He shrugged. "Not especially."

"Don't you want to get the bad guy?"

"I'm comfortable with letting the Atlanta police do that."

Exasperation merged with bewilderment. "What is wrong with you? This was your profession."

"*Was* is the operative word, Amanda. I *was* a policeman. Now I'm a farmer."

"Oh, for heaven's sake. You are not a farmer."

"Tell that to the people who buy tomatoes and peaches and onions at my roadside stand."

"You don't even grow the damned peaches." Her voice rose. That roadside stand was another bone of contention between them. Donelli regarded her coolly. She bit back another impatient jibe in an attempt to smooth the sharp edges that threatened to ruin what was left of the night. Soon, though. Soon they were going to have to explore her feelings about sitting by and watching a man she was beginning to love waste his life.

"Okay," she said so calmly her teeth ached from the effort. "I'll leave you out of this."

"It might be wise for you to stay out of it as well."

"Not on your life. I have a feeling there's a good story here and I intend to do it."

"You and your feelings. What about my feelings?"

That struck a nerve. Despite his own misgivings, he had waited patiently for her. She tucked her arm through his and gazed up at him sweetly. "What feelings are those?"

He opened his mouth, seemed about to say something, then changed his mind. Finally, he said, "I had plans for tonight."

Amanda decided not to pursue the remark he'd obviously struggled to censor. She had a hunch it was related to her pursuit of this story. "Sounds promising. Care to elaborate?"

"I was hoping to have a nice, pleasant dinner here in Atlanta, maybe stop by a club for a couple of beers and some music before we drive back home and then, who knows." There was a very interesting gleam in his brown eyes that raised goosebumps up and down her spine. It was definitely worth further investigation.

"I like the way you think, Donelli. The night is young. We can still do that."

"Amanda, the night was young when I got here. Now

it's approaching senility. The restaurant closed an hour ago."

"So we'll start with the music and then who knows." She ended on the most seductive note she could manage without feeling like Goldie Hawn trying to play Lauren Bacall.

Despite her enthusiasm, the gleam dimmed. He regarded her doubtfully. "And you won't bring up this Carrie Owens thing again for the rest of the evening?"

She grinned at him and stood on tiptoe to give him a promising kiss. "Don't expect miracles, Donelli."

CHAPTER

Two

The next morning it took Amanda almost as much effort to convince her editor, Oscar Cates, that there was a feature story in Carrie Owens's death as it had taken to get Donelli to spend the evening in a jazz club, rather than his favorite country-western bar. Neither of them adapted to change readily. *No* was their instinctive and usually adamant response to any suggestion. Then they weighed the alternatives, plodded through the possibilities, and eventually came around.

It was on days like this that she sincerely regretted suggesting that Oscar leave the weekly *Gazette* where they'd first worked together to help Joel Crenshaw start up *Inside Atlanta*. Occasionally Oscar's small-town newspaper background warred with his sound journalistic judgment and his desire for tabloid-splashy, but thorough coverage. Today was obviously one of those days.

''What about that story on historic homes you promised me?'' Oscar demanded finally. He ran his fingers through his remaining wisps of gray hair. Then, in predictable fashion, he picked up his production schedule. From his frown, Amanda could tell he was envisioning a spread of four blank pages in the middle of the magazine.

"We have that historic homes piece slotted in for next month," he reminded her, waving the paper under her nose. "The deadline's the end of next week. Can you pull this other thing together that fast?"

"You know I can't predict that," she said with a degree of patience that astonished her. She knew the deadlines as well as he did. She rubbed her temples. It was barely nine o'clock and already she had the promise of a throbbing headache. She wondered if working for Oscar qualified her for combat pay.

"Then we've got to go with the historic homes piece," he was saying with finality. "We've already paid Larry for shooting the pictures. We can't just throw away that kind of money."

Amanda groaned. Oscar tended to be as tight fisted with *Inside Atlanta*'s money as he had been with his own at the *Gazette*. Fortunately Joel, the publisher of the magazine, had slightly more liberal views about budgeting. His oft-stated goal was a provocative, exciting regional publication. He was willing to spend what was necessary to get it. That was why he had agreed to Amanda's rather exorbitant salary demand without batting an eye.

Of course, she had made sure Joel was aware that she could easily get the same amount if she went back to New York. She had hinted that editors were clamoring for her services. It wasn't too far from the truth. After all, she had begun her career in New York. And before she'd left two years earlier, she had attained a certain amount of respect and success, including a major exposé of judicial corruption that had nearly landed her a Pulitzer.

Only her sense of duty had lured her south in the first place. After endless discussions, her husband, Mack Roberts, had accepted a professorship at the University of Georgia. Reluctantly, Amanda had gone to work for Oscar, who initially was less than appreciative of her skills. He kept her writing quilting circle roundups and rural gossip until she'd nearly bitten every one of her nails to the quick in frustration. The assignments had been only slightly more exciting than watching the azaleas bloom.

Then, in a move as slick as any Georgia Bulldog halfback's, Mack deserted her for a college sophomore. With him out of her life, she had been in the enviable position of being able to choose the location of her next job when Joel approached her. By that time she had met Donelli and he was much on her mind. Working for Joel was a way to stay in Georgia without going crazy. Joel had made the choice easier by offering not only decent money, but the relative freedom to pick her own assignments. Only Oscar stood between her and absolute autonomy, which, she noted regretfully, was a little like saying only the Rockies stood between the pioneers and the West.

She tried placating him now with logic. "Oscar, those homes have stood for a hundred years."

"Longer." The boast resounded with civic pride.

"Okay, longer," she conceded. "I doubt if they'll collapse before I can get to them. They'll just gather more dust. The pictures will hold for the next issue. This Carrie Owens story is hot."

She caught the spark of curiosity in his eyes. At last! Hot stories were something Oscar understood. Quickly, she reeled off her sales pitch. She talked about the fitness craze, the affluent young adults who were the target audience of *Inside Atlanta*'s advertisers, the emotion, the tension, the mystery.

"You've already agreed to let me work on the fitness club story. Just think about the angle we have now. It's not just a feature story, Oscar. It's news and *Inside Atlanta* is on top of it. We have the inside track." She dug out her entire repertoire of journalistic clichés. She hoped they would appeal to Oscar's somewhat narrow vision.

He blinked at the barrage. His pencil tapped on the desk. She judged from its staccato rhythm that she'd piqued his interest at last. "You're sure there's something to this? It's not just some lovers' spat?"

"Absolutely. Even if it was a lovers' spat, as you so eloquently put it, we'd still have a darn good story."

"What does Donelli say?"

"I will not repeat our personal conversations," she said with feigned indignation. She knew exactly the point he was trying to make. It had nothing to do with whispered intimacies. Oscar, however, wouldn't let it go.

"I thought he'd put his foot down after you got mixed up in that murder thing with the chef."

Amanda's chin rose to a combative angle. "Joe Donelli

does not put his foot down where my career is concerned. Stick to the point, Oscar. Do you want us to break this open or don't you?"

"Okay," he said finally. "I trust your instincts."

His faith was hard won, but touching.

"Go," he continued. "Do it. But if you don't come up with something by the end of the week, you get started on the homes. Deal?"

So much for his touching faith. "Oscar, it's already Thursday."

"Then you'll have to work fast, won't you?"

He swiveled his chair away, leaving Amanda muttering a variety of unsatisfying oaths under her breath. She shot one last frosty glare in his direction and went to find Jenny Lee. The twenty-two-year-old aspired to follow in Amanda's footsteps as an investigative reporter. For the moment, however, she served as a cross between a receptionist and newsroom clerk for the magazine. Amanda found her in the ladies' room filing her nails, a look of boredom on her face. Her expression brightened at the sight of Amanda.

"Is he going to let you do it?"

"For the next forty-eight-hours or so. I need to find Carrie's boyfriend. I've already called the club. He hasn't come in. Any idea where he might be?"

Jenny Lee tapped her nail file against her teeth. Amanda flinched at the irritating sound. "Jenny Lee!"

"What?"

"Stop with the tapping. You're going to ruin your teeth, to say nothing of what you're doing to my nerves."

"Sorry. I'm thinking."

"With your nail file?"

Guiltily, Jenny Lee tucked the offending instrument in her pocket. "If Scott's not at the club, he might be at that apartment complex where he lived with Carrie. It's only a mile or so from Weights and Measures. I think he teaches exercise classes there a couple of days a week in exchange for a break on the rent."

Amanda pictured a singles complex filled with nubile women and lecherous men. She shuddered.

"If you don't find him there," Jenny Lee said, "I don't know what to suggest. Maybe one of the guys at the club would have some ideas. I think they all hang out together or at least they did before Scott and Carrie got together. Should I call them?"

"Not yet. Let me see if I can track him down at home. I'll check in with you later."

"Isn't there anything I can do?" Jenny Lee asked.

Amanda was not immune to Jenny Lee's plaintive request. She recognized herself only a few years earlier—eager, ambitious, and enthusiastic. "You joined the club a year or so ago, didn't you? How well do you know the other female fitness advisers over there?"

Jenny Lee's eyes lit up. "One of them lives in the same apartment complex I do. We've talked a couple of times out at the pool."

"Why don't you give her a call? Tell her you can't get this business with Carrie off your mind. See if you can get her to open up a little. Maybe they were friends. Maybe she'll know if Carrie was upset about anything. Don't push it, if she seems reluctant to talk. You can always leave the door open so she'll come to you later, if there's something on her mind."

"Got it. Should I record the conversation?"

Amanda hid a grin. "I don't think you need to go that far. This is just a background talk. I'll call you after I've seen Scott."

"Thanks, Amanda."

"You bet. Just don't let Oscar catch you ignoring the phones or the filing."

The Wisteria Apartments had been built in the forties in what was then described as garden style. Each long, two-story brick building had three entrances with elaborate facades. Amanda found Scott's address, went into the foyer, then up the stairs to his apartment. No one responded to her knocks, but as she went back down the stairs a small, round woman wearing a flowered housecoat opened the door of the apartment directly below Scott's and poked her head out. She had rollers in her gray hair and fifty years' worth of wrinkles on her face. She effectively put a lid on Amanda's preconceived notions about the neighborhood. If this woman had ever taken part in a wild singles orgy, it had been thirty years ago.

"If you're looking for Scott, honey, he's over in the recreation building. It's 'round back and just past the pool. He's giving one of those exercise classes."

"Thanks."

Amanda heard the blaring music when she was only

halfway to the pool. It sounded like the same tape Carrie had been using the night before. It gave Amanda an unsettling sense of déjà vu and she wondered how Scott could bear listening to it.

She found him at the front of a large room with institutional carpeting, a wet bar, a pool table, and a couple of card tables. There were book shelves along one wall with a handful of popular fiction paperbacks in no particular order and a stack of dog-eared magazines that ran the gamut from *Fortune* to *Family Circle*. The furniture, which had been pushed out of the way, was the sturdy, indestructible type chosen for function, rather than design. The exercise class was in full swing.

Scott Cambridge, when she finally took a good look at him, was a surprise. The hulking blond man with the bulging biceps was much younger than she'd expected, no more than twenty-five, maybe twenty-six. Was there enough of an age difference between him and Carrie to be the potential source of conflicts and jealousies?

At the moment he was surrounded by mostly elderly women and two geriatric men, all of whom were doing a light workout of deep kneebends and stretching exercises. He was very gentle with them, which made Amanda wish she'd been taking classes from him.

When the session was over, Amanda approached him, handing him a thick Weights and Measures towel that had been draped over a chair.

"Hi," he said with a friendly grin as he wiped perspiration from his brow. He'd obviously put considerably more energy into the workout than his students had. "One of these ladies your grandmother? We give cut rates for beautiful relatives."

Amanda smiled. The charm seemed packaged, but inoffensive. "Thanks for the compliment, but I'm already enrolled at Weights and Measures. My muscles can't handle any more stress."

He examined her more closely. "You go to Weights and Measures?"

Amanda immediately detected an insulting skepticism. She'd convinced herself that the five pounds she had gained from eating Donelli's pasta were not obvious. Apparently Scott Cambridge could locate every one of them.

"I just joined recently," she replied with a touch of defiance. "Actually I'm working on a feature story about the place."

She introduced herself. His welcoming smile faded at once, giving way to suspicion. When he spoke, his voice had turned cold. His blue eyes were the shade of a wintry sky just before visibility vanished in a blizzard of snow.

"Don't give me that feature story bullshit. You reporters are all alike, aren't you? You're a bunch of vultures. I have nothing to say to you."

He turned away. Amanda walked right back into his line of vision.

"Scott, I'm sure this is a terrible time for you. In fact, I'm a little surprised you'd be teaching today."

A muscle in his jaw worked. Pain clouded his eyes. He blinked rapidly against the shimmer of tears. Amanda felt something in her own attitude soften.

Scott's voice was barely steady as he told her, "I don't like to let these people down. They look forward to the classes. Carrie wouldn't . . ." He pulled himself together. "Well, I guess it doesn't matter what she'd have thought, does it?"

He ended on a bitter, cynical note, but his consideration for his students had sounded genuine. Her impression of Scott Cambridge improved a bit, taking him out of the category of stereotypical, empty-headed, unemotional jock, though not quite out of the category of suspect.

"Please, won't you tell me about Carrie?" she asked quietly. She saw no advantage in trying to hide her interest any longer. "I hear you two were living together. I'm sure there are things you could tell me about her that no one else could."

His expression hardened again. "I've spent the whole damned night with the police. I've had it up to here with questions," he said, even more heatedly this time. It was not an uncommon response to reporters, but Amanda made a mental note of his quick tendency toward anger anyway. There was nothing gentle about his tone now. "I told you I have nothing to say, so why don't you just get the hell out of here."

His voice had risen. The women in the class stopped their conversations to stare at Amanda, their previously curious expressions suddenly as hostile as his. The looks they directed at Scott, on the other hand, were filled with compassion and motherly protectiveness. The two men, their eyes alert, began to move closer as if ready to intercede at the first indication that Scott wanted them to.

Amanda had a vision of being knocked down and dragged out of the Wisteria Apartments by two men who reminded her of her grandfather. Oscar would love it. He'd probably find some way to work it into his "Editor's Notebook" at the front of the magazine. She took a deep breath, shot a placating smile at the men and tried again with Scott. She even risked putting a hand on his arm and felt the muscles quiver with barely controlled tension. He closed his eyes and she sensed he was struggling for calm.

"Scott, I'm not trying to do a number on you," she said persuasively. "I want to do a fair, honest profile of Carrie. More important, I want to find out why she was killed. Isn't that something you need to know, too?"

As if he could no longer sustain it, the anger seemed to drain out of him. "Look, I'm sorry I blew up, but I don't see the point. The only important thing is that she's dead. She was the best thing in my life and she's . . ." His voice broke. A convincing tear shimmered at the corner of his eye until he wiped it away. "She was the greatest. I'd never known anyone like her before."

"When did you meet?"

He hesitated, then finally shrugged in resignation. Amanda pulled her notebook out of her purse. "Okay?"

"Yeah. What the hell. We met about six months ago, when she first came to work at the club. We hit it off right away. She didn't treat me like some dumb jock."

Amanda felt a twinge of guilt. "Were there any problems over the age difference?"

"Why should there be?"

"It happens. You're a very attractive young man. You spend your days surrounded by women."

"And not a one of them could hold a candle to Carrie. I was in love with her."

Amanda retreated in the face of his obvious sincerity. He hadn't struck a false note. "When did you begin sharing an apartment?"

"About five weeks ago. I wanted her to move in here sooner, but she said she had some things that had to be tied up before she could make that kind of a commitment."

"What sort of things?"

"I'm not sure. I think there was an old relationship that wasn't quite over. It wasn't that she was seeing anyone else. I know she wasn't. But she'd get these calls sometimes and afterward she'd get really quiet. She never wanted to talk about them."

"Do you think those calls might have been linked to her death?"

"Like I said, she didn't talk about them."

"But you said she seemed quiet. Did she seem afraid, unhappy, what?"

He studied Amanda closely and seemed to come to some sort of a decision. "You want the truth?"

"Naturally."

"This didn't come from me," he said, his voice dropping to a whisper. There was an edge to the remark that Amanda identified as genuine fear. It was especially surprising in a man who seemed physically equipped to take on just about any adversary. "I didn't tell the police and if it comes out with my name linked to it, I'll swear you're lying."

"No problem."

"I think Carrie was onto something."

The statement was made as dramatically as a bad line in a B-movie, but it had the ring of truth—or at least conviction—to it. "Like what?" Amanda asked.

He shook his head. "I don't know. I've gone over it and over it, but I can't figure it out. She kept telling me there was something not quite right at the club, but she never went any further than that. I'm not sure if the calls were related to that or not. I mean it's not like she ever said anything right after the calls. They could have been from an ex-lover just as easily. At the time, I thought the stuff about the club was all in her imagination. I've been there a couple of years now and I've never noticed anything."

His face twisted in pain. He gazed at Amanda helplessly. "Damn it, why didn't I believe her? I might have been able to prevent this."

Amanda felt sorry for him. He was wrestling with tremendous grief and guilt, a devastating combination that could eat away at the good memories until none were left.

"You can't be sure of that," she consoled. "It's pointless even to think about it. Was last night any different? Was she more afraid? More tense than usual?"

Scott shook his head. "I don't think so. We don't hang out together when we're at the club. It doesn't look good, you know. I left about six. She was just starting class."

"Did you come back here?"

"Not right away. I stopped at the coffee shop down the street from the club to grab a sandwich. I got back here about eight. The police came by about an hour after that."

Amanda made a note about the alibi. She'd have to check it out. For now, though, she had nothing more to ask Scott. "You can do me a favor," she told him as she put her notebook back in her purse. "Keep your eyes and ears open around there. If you find out anything, let me know."

He nodded.

"One last thing. As far as anyone else knows, I'm only working on a feature story about Weights and Measures and other fitness clubs in the area. I think it's best for now if no one else knows I'm especially interested in Carrie's death."

"Yeah. No problem." He didn't even look up.

She gave him her card, but she doubted if he was even aware of taking it. His head was bent and his shoulders were shaking. She touched his shoulder gently, then left him to mourn alone. The handful of stragglers from his class closed ranks as she left the room.

When she got back to the office, Donelli was waiting for her, his feet on the desk, the last of her jelly beans in his hand. She rescued two of them for herself.

"What brings you into Atlanta today?" she inquired. "No out-of-control weeds to kill? No evil insects to be eradicated?"

"I was not bored, if that's your point."

"Oh, what then? Did you have to pick up some of those cute little baskets for your tomatoes?"

"Cut the sarcasm, Amanda. I didn't leave home. I came to see you. There's a slight, but distinct difference. As a purveyor of words, I'm sure you can figure it out."

"I'd like to think it's because you can't resist my body. . . ."

"Unless I dreamed last night, you know I can't."

She grinned at him. "I seem to recall something like that."

Suddenly the teasing gleam in his eyes vanished. Her grin faded.

"But that's not why you're here."

"Not exactly. I just got to thinking about this Carrie Owens thing. I checked with the police. They've ruled it a murder. She was definitely suffocated. When I called to let you know, Oscar said you were already out snooping around, so I decided I'd better get over here."

Amanda's hopes for Donelli's future as a policeman rose. She decided, however, on a little reverse psychology for a change. "I am perfectly capable of conducting my own investigation." There was a calculated note of huffy indignation in her voice.

"I know that. But would you object to a little unofficial assistance?"

She hesitated and studied him as if trying to make up her mind about his real intentions. "Do you actually plan to assist me, or serve as my bodyguard?"

He looked chagrined by her prompt detection of his motive. "Can't I do both?"

The ardent feminist in her started to decline the clearly macho offer, but the image of Carrie Owens lying on the tile floor in that steam room dimmed her noble intentions. Scott Cambridge's ominous hints added vivid color to the image. The thought of Donelli back in uniform was infinitely more appealing. It was worth a tiny sacrifice of her pride to see that happen.

"Fine," she said. "How do you feel about aerobics classes?"

He regarded her warily. "As a concept, I'm all for them. Why?"

She tucked her arm through his. "Then you'll love what I have in mind for you."

CHAPTER Three

Donelli did not love Amanda's idea.

She could tell because he was casting accusing looks in her direction with every leg kick. He'd used every tactic imaginable to convince her to let him ask the questions, while she took the class. Only her reminder that his running shorts and sweatshirt were always in the car, while hers were at home some fifty miles away, had made him finally agree to go along with her plan.

"All right," he'd conceded reluctantly as they drove toward the club. "If you're going to talk to this Jackson Greybar guy, then stick to your original story."

"But . . ."

"It's pointless not to, Amanda. Jackson already knows you're a reporter. He's going to be on guard with you. In fact, I'm surprised he didn't cancel the interview. When you finish with him, make a point of seeking out the singles. He'll probably keep an eye on you. He may even want to stick with you, so only ask people why they chose this particular club. Steer clear of direct questions about Carrie, unless they mention her name or the aerobics class. Then you can ask whatever you like. It'll be in a less threatening context and it won't arouse Jackson's suspicions."

"Thank you, Dan Rather," she mocked. "Coming from a man whose trademark is the direct approach, I find your advice a little disconcerting."

"Damn it, Amanda, I'm just trying to keep you safe."

"You want me to go back to covering quilting circles. That's what you really want."

He sighed heavily. "Okay. Maybe that is what I really want, but I respect your right to make a choice about your career. I just don't want you to take any unnecessary chances."

She glanced at him and caught the troubled expression in his eyes. The knot of tension that had begun to form in her shoulders eased. "Okay, Donelli. You're probably right. I admit at first I thought it would be best to go on pretending that I'm only interested in the singles angle, but I don't like sneaking around that way. It doesn't feel right. Besides, it'll take too long. Oscar's breathing down my neck to pull this story together practically overnight."

"Forget Oscar. Forget the deadline. Think about protecting yourself for a change. If you go charging in there with your tape recorder . . ."

"I don't use a tape recorder."

"Okay, your notebook. Same difference. If you're waving it under people's noses and asking about Carrie, someone just might get nervous and decide to eliminate one risk factor. I realize my way will require a little more subtlety and patience than you're used to demonstrating. . . .''

He did not have to draw her a picture. She got the idea. ''I am perfectly capable of subtlety and patience,'' she replied huffily. Donelli's eyebrows rose.

''When I have to be,'' she amended. ''Okay. I promise I'll do it your way. And what will you be doing, while I'm wasting time dancing around the real story?''

''I'll go the undercover route you wanted me to. I'll try to blend in, listen to what people are saying. Carrie's death is bound to be the hot topic today. Don't worry about me. It'll be a snap. I used to do this sort of thing all the time, remember?''

Amanda was thrilled that Joe remembered, even if it didn't seem to be with much enthusiasm. She thought it would be wise to refrain from comment. ''Don't forget that you need to sign up for an aerobics class right away,'' she had said instead. ''The classes will probably be jammed this afternoon, since the club was closed this morning as a tribute to Carrie.''

''How could I possibly forget the aerobics class? I still don't see why I can't skip that and just hang out.''

''Because the people in that class are the ones most likely to be talking about Carrie.''

''True, but I'm going to stick out like a sore thumb. There are nothing but women in those classes. Men do not—''

Amanda slammed on the brakes before he could finish his sentence. Despite his generally enlightened attitude, occasionally Donelli came out with a remark left over from the Dark Ages. She felt obligated to protest.

"If you value our still-tenuous relationship, don't finish that sentence. Men do take aerobics. Some of them can even keep up with the women," she'd added smugly.

Donelli groaned. She ignored it and kept right on. "Besides, don't you think it'll be interesting to see who's taking over for Carrie? Maybe it'll be someone with raging ambition who knocked her off to get the best classes."

Donelli didn't deign to respond. He was too busy rubbing his shoulder where the seat belt had snapped into it when Amanda hit the brakes.

Now, while she followed his instructions and pursued her original story about singles and fitness clubs with the other Weights and Measures co-owner, Donelli was huffing and puffing with a bunch of extraordinarily attractive women. Staring through Jackson Greybar's office window onto the main floor of the center, she counted exactly twenty-four women in the class . . . and Donelli. Every one of the women looked so svelte in a leotard that Amanda suffered a momentary pang of regret about insisting he take the class. Maybe she should have agreed that he should just lift weights and keep an eye on things. Right now, the only thing he seemed to be observing with keen interest was the rather voluptuous torso of the woman beside him.

"Miss Roberts?"

She forced her attention back to the man behind the desk. Jackson was staring at her, a puzzled expression on his almost perfect face. There weren't even any fine little crinkles at the corners of his shifty eyes. Then, again, he probably never laughed.

"You seem distracted," he said.

Amanda cursed herself. Just as Donelli had anticipated, Jackson had been reluctant to see her this afternoon. In fact, his secretary said she'd tried to call Amanda to postpone their appointment "in view of the tragic event last night."

Fortunately, Amanda had already been en route. Even after her arrival, Jackson had tried to beg off, but it was much more difficult to refuse the interview when she already had one foot in his door and a winning smile on her face. Now that she was seated across from him, she didn't think he was broken up about Carrie's death. There were no dark circles under sleepless eyes, no hint of tears. She hadn't forgotten that he hadn't even shown up last night when the club was being searched by the police. It seemed a little suspicious that he wasn't more upset over the loss of one of his most popular fitness advisers.

"I'm sorry," she apologized now. "I couldn't help watching the aerobics class. The routine is so different from the one I've been taking. Is the instructor new?"

"No. Shana has actually been with us since we opened. She usually handles the morning and afternoon classes. That's probably why you haven't seen her before. You've been coming in the evening and Carrie did all of those classes."

Amanda nearly smiled at the ease with which she'd guided the interview in the direction she wanted. "Who'll do the evening classes now?" she asked.

"For the time being Shana has agreed to take them on."

"Not permanently?"

"No. It's going to be difficult for her as it is. She has a son who's in some sort of preschool during the day. She'll have to find a baby-sitter for him when she's here in the evenings. We don't keep our day-care center open after five. As a single mother, she's not crazy about leaving her son with a stranger. Robert and I have promised her we'll find a replacement for Carrie as quickly as possible. We already have a couple of candidates in mind."

With poor Carrie not yet in her grave, something about the remark struck Amanda as callous. "With the atmosphere you've created here, I imagine you have people coming in all the time looking for work," she began cautiously.

"Not as many as we'd like. Oh, we have people who are interested, but finding someone who's both dedicated and qualified is more difficult. You were in Carrie's class. You could see the effect she had on people. She was able to motivate them in a way that's rare."

"How soon do you expect to have a replacement?"

"I'd say by the end of next week."

She stared at him. Only eight days? So much for the complexity of the hiring process . . . unless, of course, the search had begun even before Carrie's death, in anticipation of it? Amanda resolved to stop off at the library and go through the help wanted ads in recent issues of the Atlanta papers.

As if he sensed that he'd made a tactical blunder, Jackson began a litany of Carrie's irreplaceable strengths. His southern drawl, barely discernible up to now, was suddenly thick. Amanda thought it lacked sincerity, but then half the time she couldn't understand the accents in the South, much less judge the level of candor. Since he was essentially echoing Robert's comments, she supposed there was no real reason to doubt him.

When she glanced up from her notebook, Jackson was standing. She noted the Gucci belt and the Italian-cut slacks. She'd already jotted a reminder to herself about the monogrammed cuff on his silk shirt and the heavy gold chain on his left wrist. Compared to Robert's usual shorts and tank tops, Jackson was decked out for a corporate penthouse. He also looked as though the closest he ever got to a barbell was this office. He had the sort of wiry build that usually resulted from an excess of nervous energy, rather than exercise.

"If that's all, Miss Roberts?"

Actually, she hadn't even gotten started, but she recognized a dismissal when she heard one. She started for the door, then turned back. It was a technique she'd learned from watching "Columbo" reruns. "By the way, when did you hear about Carrie's death?"

"Not until quite late last night," he said without a moment's hesitation.

"You were out, then, when one of the instructors tried to reach you?"

He gave her a knowing smile. "Yes, I was."

If he meant to be coy, he was succeeding. As far as establishing an alibi, his response was less than illuminating. He'd left her no opening to pursue without arousing suspicions about her motives. She wondered if the police had had better luck. Reluctantly, she thanked him.

"Are any of the regular singles here at this hour?" she asked.

He joined her at the window and glanced around the gym. "None I recognize. It's much too early. As you can tell from the noise in our day-care area, we have mostly mothers here in the afternoon. Singles should start arriving by five o'clock or so." He placed a hand in the middle of her back and guided her toward the door. His touch made her skin crawl. "If you want to check back with me then, I'll introduce you to several."

Suddenly nervous, she forced a smile. "I may have to get back to the office before that. If we don't do it tonight, I'll be back."

"Whatever you like."

As she headed for the snack bar to go over her notes and wait for Donelli, she could feel Jackson's hard gaze following her. She sensed that, beneath all his cordiality and cooperativeness, there lurked an unspoken hostility. It made her shiver.

Since stress always made her hungry, she took a seat at the counter and studied the self-consciously healthy menu. It was heavy on carrot juice, sprouts and tofu. Naturally, it made her long desperately for a gooey hot fudge sundae with extra whipped cream. She settled for a peach yogurt drink with the promise of only 150 calories. She would sneak a handful of chocolate jelly beans to go with it.

"You must be a new member," said the pretty, dark-haired, dark-eyed woman behind the counter who brought her a glass of water. Her low voice bore a slight trace of what was probably a Hispanic accent. Amanda had seen her on previous visits. She always seemed to be engaged in animated conversations with the customers. She'd even seen her once in the women's lounge area puffing on a forbidden cigarette. She'd stubbed it out the minute she'd realized she wasn't alone. Amanda wondered now if she recalled the incident.

"Do you keep track of everyone who belongs?" she asked. The woman could prove an invaluable source if she knew everyone and was prone to gossiping.

"Just about. It's not that hard. Sooner or later almost everyone stops in here. Besides, faces are a hobby of mine. I sketch them when I have the time."

"Are you any good?"

She grinned. "If I were, would I be working here?"

Amanda grinned back. "Well, you're right. I am a new member. Amanda Roberts."

"And I am Alana Marquez."

"You have a lovely accent. What is it?"

"My parents and grandparents are Cuban. I have grown up here, but we still speak Spanish at home."

"I envy you. I've always wished I were bilingual."

"Not everyone feels as you do," she said.

"I know. I've read about the English-only legislation all over the country."

Alana shrugged. "People are sometimes afraid of what they don't understand. It's not so hard for me. I've spoken English almost all my life, but for my parents . . . they feel this hostility. It's even harder for my grandparents. They are old. They cannot change so easily."

"I took Spanish in college, but I've never really had a chance to use it."

Alana grinned. "Then we will have lessons. When you come in here after your workouts, you will speak Spanish with me. Have you taken your class today?"

"No. I've been in Carrie's class in the evenings."

"*Madre de Dios.*" Alana's expressive features immediately assumed a troubled mask. "It is very sad what happened to her. She was very young to die."

"Yes, she was. Did you know her well?" This was the perfect chance to test Alana's insights and her willingness to share them.

"Not so well. She was a lady who kept to herself. Do you think it was her heart?"

Amanda recalled Donelli's report, but knew Alana would find it odd that she knew the cause of death. "The police will have to decide that," she said evasively.

Alana leaned forward conspiratorially. "You know what I think? I told Frank just last week, I told him she was one unlucky lady. I can tell these things."

"Why unlucky?"

"She knew too much. That can bring bad luck."

The echo of Scott's theory made Amanda's fingers itch to reach for her notebook. She decided, though, that this was one conversation that would have to stay unrecorded. She didn't want to frighten the talkative Alana into silence.

"Then you think she might have been murdered? What is it you think that she knew?"

"*No sé*. I don't know," she said in a whisper, casting a fearful glance in the direction of the office. "Something here is not quite right. There is much shouting. All the time the shouting. It is not good. You know what I mean?"

"Not exactly. Who was shouting?"

"Jackson and that partner of his. Roberto." The name came out in a low hiss of dislike.

"What is it about Robert that you don't like?"

"He puts the make on all of us. Even me and he knows I am a married woman."

"You mean sexual harassment?"

"*Sí*. That is it. Sexual harassment."

That was an interesting twist Amanda hadn't counted on. Robert always had one of the lovely instructors hanging on his arm, yet despite his well-toned physique he struck Amanda as having about as much sex appeal as a flounder. Maybe he had used his position as owner to demand such devotion. Perhaps Carrie had rejected his advances more emphatically than he liked and he'd gotten his revenge. She made a mental note to get back to that before she wound up her conversation with Alana.

"Have you ever heard what he and Jackson are arguing about?" she asked.

"Never. But there is a problem, believe me, and it is his doing. You can bet on it. He is no good, that one."

"Was he interested in Carrie?"

"She wore a skirt, didn't she? With him, that is all it takes."

"Alana!" The voice from the man at the end of the snack bar carried a note of warning.

Alana rolled her eyes and shrugged. "Frank thinks I gossip too much. Maybe so, but I know how to keep my mouth shut when it matters."

She turned and said something in rapid, emotional Spanish, obviously counting on the fact that Amanda's knowledge of the language was too sketchy to keep up. Unfortunately, it was a safe bet. Amanda wasn't even able to distinguish where one word ended and another began.

Alana moved on to another customer, just as Donelli came to join Amanda. He was wearing his faded jeans and his favorite blue-striped polo shirt again. From the scowl on his face, she gathered he still wasn't overjoyed about his workout, so she refrained from mentioning it.

"Did you learn anything from any of the members?" she asked instead.

"Everyone's buzzing about Carrie's death, naturally."

"Any interesting speculation?"

"Not about that. To hear everyone talk, she was the greatest aerobics instructor since Jane Fonda."

"Even Jane Fonda has her detractors," Amanda reminded him.

"But she's still making exercise tapes. Carrie's not."

"I love it when you're subtle, Donelli. What else did you hear?"

"There's a rumor that this place might be in financial trouble. A couple of stockbroker types were discussing it in the sauna."

"If they were in the sauna, how do you know they were stockbroker types? Surely, they weren't wearing their pinstriped suits."

Donelli looked put upon. "They were wearing towels. All I had to do was listen to them, Amanda. They were discussing the club as an investment possibility. As the dollar figures went higher, the gleam in their eyes got brighter. It was definitely stockbroker talk."

"Interesting. Did they have any proof about the club's financial situation?"

"Nothing concrete. One of them did say that there's been a lot of pressure lately on people to sign up for lifetime memberships."

Amanda sipped her peach yogurt drink and grimaced. For all the taste it had, she might as well have ordered the carrot juice. Worse, the only jelly beans she could find in her purse were lime. She left them for later.

"Does that make sense to you?" she said finally. "Admittedly, I'm no financial whiz, but wouldn't that be counterproductive? It would bring in a chunk of cash now, but what about the long haul?"

"The long haul wouldn't matter, if they've socked away all that cash. It would be earning a tidy sum in interest for them."

"I still think that's too shortsighted. Once this place gets overcrowded, people will start choosing other clubs. Nobody's going to wait in line to use the exercise bike or stay in an aerobics class that's so crowded you can't move."

"They will if it's the hottest spot in town. Isn't that the whole point of your story? If fitness clubs are the in thing for singles, then singles will do whatever they have to to join the right club. You've said yourself that Carrie's class was jammed and getting bigger. Besides, if all that mattered was fitness, they'd just go to the YMCA."

"Maybe," she said, getting to her feet.

Donelli grabbed her yogurt drink like a starving man. He grimaced after the first swallow and put it back. "How can you drink this stuff?"

"As you'll notice, I didn't," she responded distractedly.

"Amanda, what are you thinking?"

"I was just wondering what the books would show."

Donelli's shoulders tensed visibly. "Oh, no, you don't," he said as she started back into the main part of the club. He put a firm hand under her elbow. When she tried to return to the office, he steered her straight toward the exit. "You are not going to try sneaking into the office for a look at the books."

She smiled demurely. "Of course not. I thought you could do that."

CHAPTER
Four

Donelli stared at Amanda for a full minute before he exploded. "Are you out of your mind? I am not going to break into the office, Amanda. No way. Forget it. You want to see the books, you go through proper channels. You get a subpoena."

"On what grounds, Donelli? I don't have any real evidence. Besides, I'm not a policeman or a lawyer."

"Then tell a policeman or a lawyer what you suspect and let him decide if it's enough to go after the books."

"I have told a policeman."

"No, you haven't!" He swallowed hard and lowered his voice. "No, Amanda. I am not a policeman and I am not breaking into that office. Am I making myself clear?"

She nodded meekly. The effort nearly choked her.

Just in case the message needed reinforcing, Donelli expressed his displeasure with her idea as they drove across town to the *Inside Atlanta* office. The vocabulary varied, but the theme remained constant. He repeated his emphatic refusal, adding a few comments about professional ethics—hers and his—the legalities and the overall morality of it. Donelli was incredibly tiresome when he was right.

"Okay," she said agreeably as she got out of the car.

"It's against the—" He paused and frowned. "Okay?"

"That's right. If you don't want to do it, I understand. It is illegal."

"That's right. It is illegal, not to mention dangerous."

"I said okay, Donelli. We'll just drop it."

As they walked from the parking garage into the skyscraper which housed the magazine's offices, he watched her as if he couldn't quite figure out the catch. Finally his gaze narrowed. "What are you thinking, Amanda?"

Her blue eyes assumed their most innocent expression. "What do you mean? I'm agreeing with you. It's as simple as that. You don't want to break in. It goes against the cop code of ethics. No problem."

She tossed her purse on her desk and went to look for Jenny Lee, leaving Donelli staring after her in consternation.

She heard him muttering to Oscar as she left the room.

"I will never understand that woman," he said as if it were a woeful inadequacy on his part.

"Join the club."

Amanda chuckled. Maybe it was worth giving up her brainstorm to have Donelli admit she was an enigma to him.

"What are you so pleased about?" Jenny Lee inquired when she found her. "Did you figure out the killer?"

That put a damper on her amusement. "Hardly. I don't

even have a solid string of suspects yet. Everybody I've talked to claims to have loved the woman. So far, I haven't come up with one single logical reason to doubt them."

"Forget logic," Jenny Lee suggested. "Any gut-level instincts?"

Amanda felt like hugging her. She was a woman after her own heart. Unfortunately, her instincts seemed to be failing her as well.

She wasn't exactly wild about either Robert or Jackson, but there wasn't a shred of evidence against them unless she counted Alana's off-the-cuff remarks about their arguments, which might not have had anything to do with Carrie. As for Scott Cambridge, he had a temper, but he also seemed to have been genuinely crazy about Carrie. The alibis were far from airtight. Jackson's was nonexistent. For the moment, though, the only one she could check out was Scott's. She would stop in the coffee shop where he claimed he had dinner the next time she was on that side of town.

"Nothing," she admitted finally. "I've got a bunch of damn threads, but I can't find the pattern. How about you? Any luck with your friend?"

"She said she'd been worried about Carrie lately, that Carrie had something on her mind."

"Scott said the same thing. Did this woman have any idea what it was about?"

"No. She said she'd seen Robert Barnes putting the make on Carrie a couple of times, but she really didn't think that was it."

"Alana said something about him being a real lecher. How did Carrie handle him?"

"She said she was cool about it. She just laughed and brushed him off. My friend said Robert took it pretty well, too. She said if there were hard feelings, she didn't see any evidence of them."

Amanda sighed. "How tight is your friend with Robert and Jackson? What does she think about them?"

"She was at the club before they took it over. My feeling is she works for them because the pay is decent. I don't think she likes them much. Why?"

"Do you think she'd tell you if there's been anything strange going on at the club since they took it over or will she be worried about her job?"

Jenny Lee laughed. "You'll have to meet Shana. I don't think she worries about much of anything."

Amanda's pulse leapt. "Shana? The other aerobics instructor?"

"Yeah. Why?"

"Because that is not the image Jackson painted of her. He told me she had a kid she's trying to support, that she hates taking on the evening class."

"That may be true. She does have a child and she's really good with him. She probably would hate working evenings. I just meant that she's not a classic type-A personality. She's real laid-back."

"I still think I ought to meet her. Can you arrange it? It needs to be someplace away from the club. Maybe this weekend at your apartment?"

"Sure, but what did you mean about something going on at the club?"

"I'm not sure." She explained about Scott's hunch and Alana's comments. "Combine those with the rumors Donelli heard about the place being in financial trouble and you might end up with a motive for murder."

"How are you going to check it out?"

She sighed. "I was going back to the club to take a look at the books, but Donelli has discouraged the idea."

"Why? It sounds like a great idea to me."

Amanda laughed. "Let me count the ways. It's illegal, unethical, dangerous, and quite probably ridiculous. If there is something going on, they'd probably be smart enough to hide it."

Jenny Lee was looking at her oddly. "But you're going to do it, anyway, aren't you?"

Apparently Jenny Lee had heard something in her voice, which even Amanda had not been aware of herself until that moment. She nodded. "If I can shake Donelli loose for a couple of hours, I am."

"Where is he now?"

"In with Oscar. They're drinking scotch and discussing the idiosyncrasies of women."

"If you really want to go, I could make sure he stays there for an hour or two."

The idea tempted. "No," she said reluctantly. "It would never work. The minute Donelli realizes I've disappeared, he'll get suspicious and come chasing after me. A bulldozer wouldn't be able to hold him back, much less you. I'll figure out another way."

"At least I could warn you he was on his way."

"How?"

"I'll just call the club and have you paged."

"And alert the whole world that I'm there? I don't think so."

"You don't have to answer the page. Just get out when you hear it."

"It could work," Amanda said thoughtfully. "And I really do want to see those books."

"Then, go."

She grinned. "Jenny Lee, I think you definitely have what it takes for this business."

"You mean a devious mind?"

"Exactly. Just one thing, though. When you call, page yourself. If anyone discovers later that the books have been touched, they might recall hearing my name and put two and two together. Do you have your exercise stuff with you?"

"In the cabinet behind my desk."

"Mind if I borrow it? Mine's at home."

"No problem." She ran back to the main office and returned in less than five minutes. "They're still talking. They didn't even notice me. Now get out of here before Donelli comes looking for you."

"Thanks, Jenny Lee."

The crowd at Weights and Measures had dwindled down to a handful of exercise nuts. The air smelled of a day's worth of sweat-dampened towels. There was no sign of

Jackson. She tugged on Jenny Lee's leotard, which was one size too small, then worked out until she saw the lights in the offices begin to go off. Only one remained on. One, damn it. The minutes kept ticking by—ten, fifteen, thirty. Each minute that passed increased the risk that Donelli would discover her absence and come tearing after her. It seemed to take forever before Robert finally left, carrying a briefcase that seemed incongruous with his shorts and tank top. Amanda breathed a sigh of relief.

Only one fitness adviser remained on duty. He was reading a bodybuilding magazine, his sneaker-clad feet propped on the reception desk, his back to the entrance to the office suite. Her heart thumping, Amanda started to slip past him. At any second she expected him to look up and catch her. Apparently, though, he was so engrossed in his study of pectorals and biceps that a herd of elephants could have thundered by without detection.

That didn't mean he wouldn't discover her at any moment, Amanda thought with a twinge of skin-prickling anxiety. It would be difficult to explain what she was doing. Breaking and entering was not on the list of prescribed exercises at Weights and Measures. In fact, under the wrong circumstances, the side effects could be downright unhealthy. Some instinct told her these circumstances fit that likelihood. She would have given almost anything to have Donelli in the room with her. Even at his bossiest and most indignant, he was a reassuring presence.

She was just about to open the top drawer of the file cabinet, when a hand clamped down on her shoulder. Her pulse skittered wildly and visions of prison cells danced in her head, followed immediately by more suffocating possibilities.

"What the hell do you think you're doing?" Donelli hissed furiously.

Relief washed over her as she whirled around. It was short-lived. The expression on Donelli's face, a mixture of anger and betrayal, was not reassuring.

"Thank goodness," she said with shaky bravado. "I can use an extra pair of hands."

"You could do with a horsewhipping."

"Sounds kinky, if you ask me."

"Amanda, this isn't funny. Didn't you hear a single thing I said to you earlier?"

"All of it."

"Then what in God's name made you do this? You promised me that you'd given up on the idea."

She sighed. "I know. You have every right to be furious, but could we discuss my shortcomings a little later? Right now, I'd like to go through these files before someone else decides to join us."

"We're leaving now."

She shook her head. "You go. I'm in here now and I'm not going until I have what I came for."

"So help me, Amanda."

"Later, Donelli."

Their gazes clashed, hers stubborn and defiant, his equally determined. "I am not leaving, Donelli, and that's final. You can go or stay."

"I'll stay," he said finally, "but you and I are going to have a very long talk about trust when this is over."

She had never heard his voice so cold or seen his expression so disapproving. The chill wrapped itself around her heart as she remembered the last time she'd seen a look like that. The look had been her own as she stared in the mirror after Mack had told her about his sophomore lover.

"I'll make it up to you. I promise," she whispered.

"I'm not sure you can, Amanda."

Gut-wrenching fear of the emotion she had seen in Donelli's eyes combined with her nervousness. She began to chatter nonsensically, anything to keep that awful silence from building into a tension they would never overcome.

"How about dinner when we're done here?" she offered. "How do you feel about linguini with clam sauce? Maybe a little garlic bread, a nice bottle of red wine?"

Pasta and wine always put him into a mellow mood. He was only one generation out of Rome. The aroma of garlic practically transformed him. It reminded him of a brownstone in Brooklyn and a mother who spent countless hours standing in front of a stove to feed a family of eight. There were five more Donelli sons and if all of them had appetites like Joe's, their grocery bills must have been astronomical. At the moment, however, the prospect of Amanda's linguini seemed to be having little effect on him.

"Amanda, I've eaten your pathetic excuse for Italian food. You cook it as if you were feeding a bunch of Englishmen with stomach ulcers. There's no soul in it. Now will you get out of my light so I can see what I'm doing."

She moved a few paces back. "You don't have to get nasty. The only thing I cooked as a kid was hamburgers. Mack did the cooking when I was married."

"How much skill does it take to chop up some clams and garlic and boil a little linguini?"

"Okay. Okay. Forget it. I'll take you out for dinner. Will you just hurry up and get into the file before somebody comes along and wonders what we're doing back here."

"You want to pick the lock, be my guest. If you'll recall, this wasn't my idea."

"I want you to pick it. I just want you to do it faster."

"I could just pry the damn thing open with my Swiss army knife. It'll look like a can of tuna when I'm done, but what the heck?"

"Don't be a wiseass, Donelli."

Thankfully, the lock clicked softly. The file drawers slid open with ease to reveal . . . nothing. Absolutely nothing.

"Now what, Miss Marple? Any idea where else they might hide the books?"

"You used to investigate crimes for a living," she reminded him. "But since you're asking me, my guess would be the desk or the credenza."

"Since that's the only other furniture in here aside from the chair, I'd have to say you're very perceptive. You go through the credenza. I'll work on the desk."

Amanda ignored the sarcasm. Donelli tended to get a little short-tempered when he was breaking the law. She found it encouraging. It proved you could take the badge off the detective, but you couldn't take the detective out of the man. She allowed herself a tiny smirk of satisfaction. It vanished when she recalled the likelihood that he was going to wring her neck once they got out of here.

She knelt in front of the credenza, offering a prayer of thanks for the absence of locks. Filled with anticipation, she slid open the door at one end of the long, low metal cabinet. It moved noiselessly on its track to reveal a neatly arranged stack of fluffy, white hand towels. The center section contained a box of herbal tea bags, a jar of honey, a dirty spoon, and three mismatched cups, one of them chipped.

"So far I'm not impressed with his filing," she commented. "What about you? Anything in the desk?"

"Lint."

Amanda's head snapped around at that. "Not even a scrap of paper?"

"Not so far. The man must have memorized the phone directory, too. There's no address book, no Atlanta directory. Nothing."

Amanda opened the final door on the credenza. "Well, I found the phone book and a Rolodex." She removed the latter and twirled it around. "Blank cards. It must have been a gift when they opened the place. It's certainly never been in use."

She sat back on her heels, mystified. "Do you suppose he just emptied the place out?"

"Why would he do that?"

"Maybe he's a neatness freak. Maybe he's planning to skip town. How would I know? It just doesn't make sense for an office that's in use to be this clean. There's not even a used tea bag in the garbage."

"You're sure Robert uses this office? Maybe he shares the one next door with Jackson."

"Then who the hell uses this one? The maid?"

"Don't get testy, Amanda. Let me check out the closet and then we'll look next door." He opened the door. "Well, well, what have we here?"

Amanda was on her feet at once, trying to peer past Donelli's broad shoulders which were more effective in blocking her view than blackout curtains. She couldn't see a damn thing. She nudged him aside. "What?"

"Another filing cabinet." He reached for a drawer. It didn't budge. "Another locked filing cabinet," he added in disgust.

"I don't suppose you saw a key, when you were going through the desk," Amanda said hopefully.

"Nope, but this should be a breeze, now that I've gotten the hang of it."

The lock gave way after Donelli's fifth attempt to pick it. The top three drawers contained members' files in alphabetical order. The bottom drawer held a set of ledgers. Bingo!

In the dim light coming in from the hallway, they went over the pages of the first book, trying to make sense of the entries. It appeared that Weights and Measures had operated in the black over the last eighteen months, but barely. Even with money tight, though, the club seemed in no danger of going under as it apparently had been when

Jackson and Robert had bought it at a reportedly rock-bottom price.

Amanda picked up the second ledger. "What do you suppose this one is?"

She opened it, held it up to the light, and, upon studying it, found that it duplicated the first book with one significant exception. The income entries had been systematically increased by anywhere from twenty-five to fifty percent. Or had the figures in the first book been reduced? Either way it appeared there was a scam involved.

"Do you suppose Carrie could have found out about this?" Amanda asked.

"It's possible. Any idea why the books might have been tampered with in the first place?"

"It appears to be an attempt to defraud someone, but who? Was Robert trying to put something over on his partner? Or was it Jackson?"

"I can answer that," a very cold voice responded.

Amanda reached instinctively for Donelli's hand. Whatever he might be feeling toward her at the moment, he held it tightly. Normally she found that very reassuring, but with her other hand caught in the cookie jar, so to speak, his touch lost some of its usual comfort.

Robert Barnes flipped on the overhead light and strolled into the office. Muscles rippling and very, very angry, he was an intimidating sight. He removed the books from Donelli's possession with a deceptively casual gesture that made Amanda cringe. Then he smiled. It was not sincere.

Still, Donelli smiled back, though his eyes remained

wary. He settled himself in a chair, crossed his legs and gestured for Amanda to do the same.

"We'd love to hear your explanation," he said so calmly Amanda felt like embracing him. However angry he might be with her, he was clearly putting it aside for the moment in favor of gathering evidence. Those books might not have gotten her off the hook for her actions, but at least they had proved her hunch right. Donelli was now reacting instinctively . . . just like a cop.

"First, indulge me just a little," Robert suggested. It bordered on an order. "What are you two doing in here?"

"Signing up for memberships," Amanda responded hopefully. Robert gave her a disbelieving stare. Even Donelli seemed a tad impatient.

"Actually, Amanda's on a pretty tight deadline for her story and just tonight she realized she hadn't gotten the statistics she needed on your memberships. You know, how many singles you have, that sort of thing. We stopped back to see if we could find them."

The lie tripped off his tongue so readily, even Amanda was almost taken in by it. She peeked at Robert and noticed that he seemed slightly more uncertain than he had been when he'd first come in. He apparently had a very low opinion of reporters. He seemed to accept the possibility that they'd routinely engage in breaking and entering just to locate a missing fact or two.

"What are you doing with the books?"

Good question, Amanda thought. She awaited Donelli's response eagerly.

"We thought there might be a notation in there of the total memberships," Donelli said.

"I see." There was a speculative gleam in Robert's eyes that Amanda didn't like. "Did you find the figures?"

"Not the ones we were looking for."

Donelli's words hung in the air. Amanda understood the implication. She wondered if Robert did. Judging from the return of that ashen tinge to his complexion, he understood perfectly. His gaze narrowed.

"Okay, let's not waste time. Why don't we talk a deal? You two get out and keep your mouths shut and I won't press charges for breaking and entering."

She had to give him credit. He didn't waste time and he didn't mince words.

Donelli nodded agreeably. "Seems reasonable. I don't suppose you'd like to satisfy my curiosity and explain the dual bookkeeping system."

"Not especially."

"Who knew about it?" he persisted in an ironically conversational tone. No third degree had ever been administered more casually. Amanda was practically overcome with admiration.

"I told you I didn't want to discuss it."

"Was this the information Carrie Owens discovered? Is this the reason you killed her?"

Red replaced the gray in Robert's cheeks. Furious, he leaned toward Donelli. "I don't like your accusations, mister. Maybe I ought to add slander to the breaking and entering charge."

"Maybe you should," Donelli said quietly. "These books would make interesting reading in court."

Robert sat back. "These books don't prove a damn thing," he said with considerably less confidence.

"Don't they?" Amanda said. "Even you have to admit this dual bookkeeping system is just the tiniest bit suspicious."

He nodded. "I'm willing to admit that. But you don't have any evidence linking it to a crime."

"Not yet," Amanda said. "But I doubt if we'd have to dig very deep to find one. We could start with Carrie's death. In fact, I have an interesting theory about that."

She settled back in her chair, enjoying herself. Now Robert was the one who appeared hunted. "I think she discovered the books, tried blackmailing you and Jackson, and you killed her to keep her quiet. Or maybe she just threatened to turn you over to the authorities. I think I like that one even better. It doesn't besmirch her image, which you warned me about just the other night."

Robert's shoulders slumped lower. "Okay, what do you really want to know?"

"Did you fiddle with the books?"

"No. It was Jackson's idea."

"And Carrie found out about it."

"No. Even if she had, the information is not enough to murder her over. If anyone around here should have been murdered over this, it was Jackson. Believe me, when I found out what he was doing, I hit the roof."

Which could explain the arguments Alana had overheard. "Was he skimming the profits?" she asked.

"What profits? That's the duplicate set of books. It's intended to impress a potential buyer of this place with its solvency."

"Then you are considering selling? Why?"

"We've had the place nearly two years now. We turned it around, made it financially sound, if not a roaring success. That's the challenge." He offered a tentative, self-deprecating smile. "I'm afraid both of us have fairly short attention spans. Fortunately, we do well enough, so we can afford to be self-indulgent."

"Then it was a mutual decision to sell?" Amanda persisted.

"Absolutely."

"If the place is such a success, why the need for the other books?"

"Jackson seemed to feel if the guy got a look at our legitimate cash flow, he'd lose interest."

"I suppose you won't mind if we talk to Jackson and your prospective buyer about this as well? What's his name, by the way?"

"Trace Weston."

Amanda whistled. "Of Weston International?"

"Yes."

Trace Weston reputedly indulged in multimillion-dollar hobbies. He operated businesses on a scale much larger than Weights and Measures. His last takeover had involved a company with assets in the billions and at least a dozen subsidiaries worldwide. Perhaps he was thinking of building a skyscraper next to the club and turning it into his private gym.

"No wonder Jackson thought you'd need big bucks to impress him."

"Can't you leave him out of this? The phony books haven't been used and they won't be."

"And Carrie, any theories about what she did find out?"

"I don't think she found out anything. I think she got herself caught up in some love triangle."

Amanda couldn't hide her skepticism. "With Scott and someone else? I don't think so."

"Scott was just an additional complication. I was talking about Frank."

"Frank?"

"Marquez. He operates the snack bar. He and Carrie were pretty tight. I used to see them together all the time."

"In the club?"

"No. They'd take their breaks together and go down to the corner coffee shop."

"Is this Frank any relation to Alana?"

Robert permitted himself a slight smile. "I think you're beginning to catch on. She's his wife."

CHAPTER

Five

A*manda* left Weights and Measures convinced of her mission's success. She felt vindicated. She had all sorts of new evidence, new pieces to the puzzle. She had only to see where they fit and then her story would fall together.

"Do you suppose Alana found out about the affair and killed Carrie?" she asked Donelli as they crossed the parking lot. "She did seem awfully anxious to throw suspicion onto Robert. Maybe she made it up to cover her own guilt."

When her speculation drew no response, she went on. "Then again, it is entirely possible that she believed what she told me. If you ask me, Jackson and Robert are unlikely partners. There was almost bound to be friction, especially after Robert found out Jackson had been tampering with the books. Do you believe they actually agreed to walk away from a successful business venture?"

Donelli sighed. "Amanda, give it a rest."

"I can't give it a rest. I only have another day before Oscar's going to want me back on that historic homes story. I need to know what you think."

"I think that you and I are going to have a very long talk when we get home and it isn't going to have a damn thing to do with Robert or Jackson or Alana."

Amanda swallowed hard past the lump that formed in her throat when she met Donelli's ominous gaze. His jaw was set, his expression implacable. The ice was back in his voice. He held her car door open for her, then closed it very carefully. "I'll see you back at my place."

She tried to buy some time. She needed to think. Donelli needed to calm down. "Maybe this should wait until morning."

"Tonight, Amanda. Don't take any detours."

Normally she would have looked forward to the long drive to Donelli's house, even though she hated the dark country roads. She did some of her best thinking behind the wheel. With a little concentration she might have been able to add up the bits of new evidence. Instead, she found herself staring at Donelli's headlights in her rearview mirror and wondering whether her impetuous behavior tonight had marked the beginning of the end of their relationship. He had been impatient with her in the past. He had worried about her to the point of being bossy and overprotective. He had never been quite so furious. His eyes, which could make her weak with longing, tonight had left her trembling for a far different reason. They'd condemned her.

Her instinctive reaction was to fight back. She hadn't gotten where she was in life by being meek. She took chances. She accepted the consequences. And one consequence of tonight might very well be the loss of Donelli's respect. The prospect left her feeling very empty.

When he'd pulled into his driveway beside her, when he'd followed her into the house, when the coffee had been made and poured—all in unbearable silence—she sat across from him at the kitchen table and waited. It was his scene. She wanted to see how he'd play it.

"Why did you do it?" he asked finally.

She tried to think of an explanation he might understand, then gave up. To a man of Donelli's character, there was no justification. She settled for the truth. "I knew there were answers there that I needed."

"And you couldn't wait? You couldn't go after those answers in the right way?"

"Don't sound so self-righteous," she snapped defensively. "Did you always do everything by the book, Donelli?"

"If I could."

He didn't even hesitate, damn him. Worse, she knew he was telling the truth. "And how many cases did it cost you?"

"More than one, probably, but Amanda, there are laws. If a cop doesn't do it by the book, the case will wind up being thrown out of court anyway."

"I'm an investigative reporter, Donelli. Not a cop. I respect what you're saying. I understood why you didn't want to go. That's why I went back there tonight without you."

"Don't try to make it sound like a noble act. You were

after a story and you weren't about to let a little thing like breaking and entering or betraying a promise to me stop you from getting it."

"I didn't promise you I wouldn't go," she reminded him. "I said I wouldn't push *you* to go."

"That's a very fine line, Amanda. On a code of honor it probably wouldn't even show up."

Suddenly it was all too much for her. She was exhausted. She was tired of the guilt that had her eyes smarting with unshed tears. She slammed her cup back on the table, ignoring the splash of coffee. "Okay, Donelli, I was wrong. There. Are you satisfied? I made a mistake. I'm guilty. Where do we go from here? Do you want a scarlet *B* and *E* embroidered on all my clothes? Do you want me pilloried in the town square? What will it take?"

A tear spilled down her cheek. She brushed it away furiously. If he was going to walk out on her, she was not going to let him see her cry. She bit her lip and waited.

"An apology would do as a start," he said softly.

She looked up and met his eyes for the first time in what seemed an eternity. They had warmed again. Slightly. He reached across the table and touched her hand. Her fingers curled gratefully around his. A sigh of relief whispered through her. It went clear to her soul. She hadn't realized just how desperately scared she'd been.

"I'm sorry," she said. "I'm sorry I went back without telling you."

Resigned amusement played about his lips. "But not sorry you went?"

She wanted to say yes. She really did, because he wanted

to hear it. But the truth was that she would do it again, if she had to, and he knew it.

"No," she admitted regretfully. "I'm not sorry I went. If what we learned tonight will help to find whoever murdered Carrie Owens, then I can't be sorry about that. Despite what you may think, I'm not just in this for the glory. When I'm caught up in a story, I damn well care about the people affected, whether it's society as a whole or one individual like Carrie. It's my way of fighting injustice and sometimes, I'll admit, I play dirty. I hope to God you can live with that, because I don't think I could ever change."

He nodded slowly, his expression rueful. "I know. And I suppose a part of me wouldn't want you to. I can admire that single-minded sense of purpose, that desire to right wrongs. I identify with it. It made me become a cop. But I also know the risks it entails and when I see you taking them, it scares the hell out of me. When I realized you had left your office while I was in with Oscar, my stomach felt like somebody had dumped acid in it. I guessed right away where you had gone, but Jenny Lee wouldn't admit it. I wasted nearly ten minutes trying to get that girl to talk. She's almost as stubborn as you are."

"I'll tell her you said that. She'll consider it a compliment. That reminds me, she was supposed to signal me if you caught on. She didn't do it."

He grinned at that. "Oscar and I figured as much. He told her if she even thought about picking up a phone to warn you, she'd better plan on being a receptionist for her whole career."

"Interesting threat. It's probably the only one that could have worked."

"You never have given Oscar enough credit for his perceptiveness. By the way, he gave me a message for you."

"What?"

"He said if you were arrested to give him a call. He said he'd come down and post bail for you. He seemed to think I might not do it."

She grinned. "You're right. He is perceptive." Her expression suddenly turned serious again. She rubbed her fingers across Donelli's knuckles. "Joe, are we going to be okay about this?"

She caught the flicker of hesitation before he finally said, "As long as we're honest with each other from now on, I think we can give it a hell of a shot."

"You don't sound nearly as convinced as you might have twenty-four hours ago."

"Maybe that's because I'm just beginning to understand that sustaining a relationship is not always as easy as falling in love."

Amanda's pulse skipped a beat and then another. "It is worth it, though." It was part statement, part plea.

"Yes. It's worth it."

As his gaze locked with hers, he stood up and held out his hand. Overwhelmed by the need for reassurance, Amanda moved past the outstretched hand into his embrace. Her arms crept around his waist and her cheek settled against his chest. She could feel the steady thump of his heart, feel his warmth stealing into her. His familiar masculine scent filled her senses. With his chin resting atop her head, he sighed.

"What was that for?" she inquired in a voice gone suddenly lazy.

"Contentment. The world feels right when I have you in my arms like this."

"I can't always be in your arms."

"Then I suppose I'll just have to make the most of the moments when you are."

His lips sought hers. The slow, leisurely kiss was pure intoxication. It sent fire through her bloodstream, waking her senses to every nuance of his mouth against hers. No touch was ever as sweet as one so nearly lost, no heat as intense as one nearly extinguished. Her skin came alive to sensation—the teasing texture of cotton against her suddenly bared midriff, the hot silk of lips against her breasts.

He claimed her there, in the kitchen, her back pressed against the table, her clothes and his in a tangle around her. After the tender beginning, gentleness fled, replaced by urgent need—a need to feel, a need to reaffirm, a need to love. And when they'd found the white-hot core of passion, they basked in its glow, savoring it for as long as they could before giving in to its wild demand.

Shaken by the raw hunger that had swept them away, Amanda felt incapable of thought, much less movement. It was Donelli who saw that they got into bed. When they were stretched out on cool sheets, he drew her back against his warmth. His touch restored her faith in the future. Filled with contentment, she fell into a deep, dreamless sleep.

When she awoke, though, the tangled web of Carrie

Owens's murder was very much back on her mind. It was only four in the morning, but she knew chasing sleep was pointless. She settled her head more comfortably on Donelli's shoulder and tried to put together all the information she had gathered. She was lying there staring at the ceiling, wishing she had Donelli's perspective, when he finally woke up. She might have nudged him ever so slightly to see that he did.

"It's still the middle of the night," he mumbled sleepily. "What's wrong?"

"Nothing. I'm just thinking."

He groaned. "I don't suppose I need to ask about what."

"Does all that stuff Robert said about Trace Weston and about Jackson's tampering with the books make sense to you?"

Swearing under his breath, he reached over and switched on the lamp beside the bed. She was certain he did it just so she could see the look on his face.

"I think it is entirely possible that two businessmen, unlikely partners or not, would agree to sell a company if the price was right," he said.

"And Alana Marquez?"

"I can't say. I haven't met the lady. The first time I ever saw her was yesterday when I met you in the snack bar."

"Then why don't you spend some time with her tomorrow and see what you can find out? I'd like your impression."

"Not tomorrow, Amanda. I've already been away from the farm too much."

"Donelli," she began impatiently.

"Don't even start. This is my job, Amanda. I'll help you out when I can, but this place doesn't run itself."

It took everything in her to keep her from starting an argument. She considered playing on the threat of danger. With his protective instincts aroused, Donelli would forget all about his weeds. In the long run, though, it would be to her disadvantage. She didn't want the man hovering. She wanted him involved in the case. She wanted him to start using his brain again, instead of his back, and she knew that deep down Donelli wanted it, too. But it had to be a decision he reached on his own.

"Will you talk to her when you get some time?" she asked as a compromise.

"She saw me with you. What makes you think she'll even talk to me?"

"You're a very sexy man," Amanda said in a deliberately low purr.

Donelli rolled his eyes at the obvious flattery, then groaned as she followed the statement with a very provocative kiss. She loved the salty taste of his skin after they'd made love. She also loved the way his body responded to her lightest caress. She tried several variations until they were both breathing hard.

"That was very persuasive. I probably could get into Atlanta by midafternoon. Just how far do you want me to go with this Alana to get the information you want?" he inquired more cheerfully.

Amanda yanked on a handful of the dark hairs on his chest. "Not that far, Donelli."

He sighed again, this time in feigned disappointment. At least, she thought it was feigned. Just in case, she switched off the light and set about reminding him exactly how good they were together. When they finally fell back to sleep, the sky was already streaked with the peach and gray tones of what promised to be a spectacular dawn.

On Friday morning Amanda left Donelli riding a tractor, his shoulders bared to the sun, a sweat-streaked hat low on his brow. He looked impossibly sexy and very contented. She felt like throwing clods of the red Georgia dirt at him. She settled for speeding out of his driveway, sending swirls of dust in her wake.

On the long ride to the office she couldn't quite decide whether to start the day by paying another visit to Scott Cambridge or attempting to get an appointment with Trace Weston. She decided on the latter, hoping it would add some new pieces to the puzzle.

What it added was frustration. Her first call to Weston International linked her to an executive secretary who'd apparently received her training at a guard dog academy. She was not inclined to arrange an appointment, nor was she particularly receptive to the idea of simply putting Amanda's call through.

"I could connect you with one of his assistants, if you like."

"I don't like. It's a private matter that requires Mr. Weston's personal attention." She didn't really want the man to retreat behind the slick facade he usually assumed for the media. It would be time enough to tell him about *Inside Atlanta* when she was inside his office. Then, if he threw her out, it would be rather telling behavior.

"I also handle his personal affairs. Perhaps I can help you."

"You could help me," Amanda conceded.

The woman's frosty manner warmed to a temperature just above freezing. "Yes?"

"You could put me through to Mr. Weston."

"Ms. Roberts." The icy hauteur was back. "We have already been through this. If you change your mind about speaking to one of Mr. Weston's assistants, do call back."

The phone clicked emphatically. Amanda's blood pressure rose. She slammed her own phone down, grabbed her purse and a new supply of jelly beans, and marched through the office.

"Where are you going?" Oscar called out as she exited.

"To see Trace Weston."

"Trace Weston!" She could hear Oscar's booming exclamation all the way to the elevator. He came tearing after her, tie flapping.

"What the hell do you want with him?" he demanded as the elevator doors slid closed. Amanda smiled and waved.

Weston International occupied the top seven stories of a thirty-three-floor skyscraper in downtown Atlanta. Naturally enough, it was known as Weston Tower. She was only surprised they hadn't named the street Weston Boulevard. A liveried doorman stood at attention in front of the building. The lobby had an Italian marble floor,

Chinese urns filled with plants that wouldn't dare to drop a leaf or turn yellow, a Louis XIV security desk, and etched brass elevator doors. Mirrored walls sent her irritated reflection scowling back at her. She was not at all surprised to discover that Mr. Weston's office was on the penthouse floor. She spent the ride up trying to smooth her hair and her ruffled feathers.

When the doors opened onto the penthouse suite, they did so with a sort of hushed reverence. Amanda felt an instant awe herself. A well-known painting by Van Gogh hung on the wall behind the receptionist's desk. The vivid burst of color hit her senses as only an original could. It was all the more powerful set against the elegant, muted decor. Amanda was not easily impressed, but her mouth went dry.

Suddenly she heard a light, friendly chuckle. "It has that effect on everyone. I'm glad I get to sit with my back to it or I'd probably drool with envy all day long."

Amanda finally tore her gaze away from the painting and found herself standing in front of a sleek black woman who, like the office, embodied an understated elegance. Her linen dress was a subdued shade of blue. Pearls glistened at her throat. Her Afro haircut emphasized the perfection of her face. The only thing about her that lacked sophistication was her smile. Her eyes twinkled with impish good humor. She was definitely not the woman Amanda had spoken to earlier on the phone. A brass nameplate on her desk identified her as Reba Carlyle.

"What can I do for you?" she asked and Amanda had

the feeling she honestly meant to be as accommodating as possible.

"Any chance you can get me in to see Trace Weston?"

"You looking for a job?"

"No."

"You want to borrow money?"

Amanda grinned. "No."

"You're not filing a paternity suit, are you?"

Amanda found herself laughing. "Does that happen often?"

The receptionist winked. "I can't swear to the legitimate statistics on it, but the threat is common enough, according to the tabloids."

"Mr. Weston must lead an interesting life."

"Not half as interesting as the gossip about it."

"Well, I'm just here on business. I understand he's interested in buying a piece of property. I'm curious about why."

"You came all the way down here without an appointment just to satisfy your curiosity?"

Amanda pulled out a business card and handed it to her. At least if Weston took cover now, she'd know about it.

"*Inside Atlanta*, huh? This ought to be interesting," she said and picked up her phone.

Something in her inflection made Amanda become alert. The explosion of sound on the other end of the line added to her sense that she'd just blundered into a situation in which she was missing more facts than she possessed.

"Go on in, honey. The barracuda just inside the door will show you the way."

Even before she heard the voice, she knew the barracuda was the woman she'd spoken to on the phone. Weston didn't need more than one protector like that to run interference. She was now scowling fiercely at Amanda.

"Why didn't you tell me this morning you were from *Inside Atlanta*? Mr. Weston is a major investor in the magazine. Of course, I would have arranged for you to see him."

Amanda felt as though someone had just slugged her in the stomach. "Trace Weston owns part of *Inside Atlanta*?"

"You didn't know?" She seemed to take pleasure in Amanda's ignorance.

"No. Why isn't his name on the masthead?"

"He prefers to keep his involvement with many corporations quiet. He and Mr. Crenshaw decided it would be best to handle the magazine in that manner. Now, if you'll follow me, Mr. Weston will see you now."

Amanda followed, feeling as though she'd just stepped into the rabbit's hole in *Alice in Wonderland*. The sensation intensified when she came face to face with Trace Weston. Tall, thin, and bespectacled, he looked startlingly familiar and not just in the way any well-publicized face looks familiar. She had seen him less than forty-eight hours earlier at Weights and Measures, though without the glasses. He'd been consoling his fiancée, Felicia Grant, after the discovery of Carrie Owens's body.

She swallowed hard and held out her hand. He shook it, then gestured for her to sit down.

"What can I do for you, Ms. Roberts?"

"You can tell me about your involvement with Weights and Measures."

She couldn't be certain because of the glasses, but she thought she caught a glimmer of surprise in his eyes. "What makes you think I have any interest in it?"

"According to an informed source, you're considering buying it. Add to that the fact that I saw you there on the night Carrie Owens was killed and I'd have to say there seems to be reason to ask the question."

He laughed. "I can see why Joel wanted to hire you. You're good."

"Thanks for the compliment, but I'd rather you just answered me."

"Off the record, I'll tell you anything you want to know."

"I'm afraid that won't do. I'm working on a story. I need to be able to quote you."

"Then I guess we've reached an impasse."

Amanda could either do the diplomatic thing and retreat or risk her job by being direct. There was no choice. "Why don't you want to talk on the record, Mr. Weston? Does Felicia know more about Carrie's death than she told the police?"

His friendly expression vanished. "Felicia stays out of this entirely, Ms. Roberts, or your story will never appear."

"I repeat, what are you so uptight about?"

"Ms. Roberts, let's face facts. Any time a man in my position demonstrates the slightest interest in a company, the cost goes shooting up. People bid on it just because they figure if I want it, it must be worth having. Now I may have money to burn, but I don't like to waste it. There are places where it's better spent."

"Your philanthropy, especially at the University of Georgia, is well known, Mr. Weston. So is the range of your business interests. Weights and Measures represents pocket change to you, even if the cost goes up by a few thousand. Why do you want it at all?"

"I don't."

"But—"

He waved aside the interruption. "Felicia does. I plan to give it to her as a wedding present and I don't want her reading about it in *Inside Atlanta* before the marriage takes place in the fall."

"An interesting trinket. Wouldn't she prefer diamonds?"

"Oddly enough, no. She's a pragmatic woman. She knows I've been divorced three times already. She's not planning on being the fourth, but just in case she wants to own something that can give her an income. I figured what the hell, it's cheaper in the long run than alimony."

To her amazement, Amanda believed him. It was exactly the sort of quirky thing a man in his position might do. She was also more than a little impressed with Felicia Grant's common sense.

"Thanks for your candor," she said as she stood up to leave.

"Just keep it out of the magazine," he said, walking her to the door. "If you don't, I'll tell Joel those offers you hinted you had from New York were so much bull."

She turned pale, despite his teasing smile.

"They might have wanted you back up there, but none of the papers you mentioned had an opening when we hired you a few months back."

"If you knew that, why did you let him hire me?"

"Because I like your style. You go after what you want. Just don't make the mistake of getting in the way of something I want."

He winked and shut the door before Amanda could decide whether to tell him off or run like hell. She decided to race back to the office and tell Oscar off instead.

Less than fifteen minutes later she was standing in front of Oscar's desk. "Why the hell didn't you tell me that this magazine is owned by Trace Weston?"

"Why didn't I tell you? You're the one who introduced me to Joel Crenshaw. I assumed you knew who was bankrolling the thing."

He had a point. "Okay, but why didn't you stop me this morning before I went over there and made an utter ass of myself?"

"Think back, Amanda," he said patiently. "You inside the elevator. Me outside, screaming my fool head off. You're the one who let the damn doors close before I could say anything."

She turned around and stalked back to her desk. She hated it when Oscar made her feel about three inches tall. She took out her thirty-day membership card and dialed the number for Weights and Measures. "Is Scott Cambridge working today?"

"He's here, but he's with a member. You want me to get him?"

"That's okay. I'll come over there to see him."

She made a quick stop at the *Atlanta Constitution* to check out the help wanted ads, but there was nothing to indicate that Weights and Measures had been looking for Carrie's replacement prior to her death. So much for that theory. The stop and the long drive around the Atlanta perimeter did serve one purpose: she calmed down. She supposed it didn't really matter who owned *Inside Atlanta* as long as she was permitted to do the job they'd hired her to do. It just would have made it a whole lot simpler if she'd known all the players before she'd entered the game.

At the club she found Scott coaching a man with a hefty paunch through a series of exercises. Once again, she was impressed with his kindness and patience.

"Can I see you when you're through?" she asked as the two men moved on to the next machine.

Scott nodded. "The snack bar in fifteen minutes?"

"Let's make it the coffee shop on the corner. I'm in dire need of something rich and caloric." She was also in need of more privacy than the snack bar would give them and it would give her a chance to check out Scott's alibi.

"I'll meet you there."

He joined her twenty minutes later, just as she was guiltily finishing up a thick slice of New York cheesecake that made her nostalgic for her favorite West Side deli in Manhattan. Scott slid into the booth and ordered an extra large orange juice.

"Can't you at least order something with caffeine, so I won't feel quite so guilty?"

He chuckled. "It's your conscience. Don't make me responsible."

She responded to his easy grin with a smile of her own. "It's good to see you more cheerful."

He shrugged. "It comes and goes. I thought coming in today would be the hardest thing I'd ever done, but it wasn't. It was a piece of cake compared to climbing back into our bed last night without her beside me."

"I know what you mean," she said softly, thinking of the endless nights after Mack had left her.

"You lost somebody, too?"

"To divorce. He moved on. I wanted to burn the damn bed for a long time afterward."

They sat for a few minutes in respectful silence, consumed by their own memories. It was Scott who finally broke it. "Why'd you want to see me? Did you find out something about who killed her?"

"I'm not sure." She searched for an easy way to ask the next question, then finally decided there wasn't one. "I hate to ask you this, but how close were Carrie and Frank Marquez?"

He looked puzzled. "They were co-workers. Why?"

"I have a source who says otherwise."

Color suffused his cheeks. "Your source is wrong," he said. "There was no affair."

"If there was, it might give us a suspect."

"Who, Alana?"

"She's one possibility."

"Jesus Christ, you really are a piece of work. Unless it's got dirt smeared all over it, you're not interested. The woman was living with me. Don't you think I'd know if she was still sleeping with someone else?"

"You said yourself that there might have been another relationship, one she wasn't quite free of."

"It wasn't Frank. Carrie would never have gotten involved with a married man. I knew her. The lady had a great respect for commitment."

"That doesn't mean she might not have made a mistake along the way. We're all capable of doing that."

"I would have known."

Amanda bit her lip, debating whether to ask the one last question that had to be answered. "Are you sure you didn't?"

As the implication sank in, Scott stared at her with eyes filled with betrayal. Not Carrie's betrayal, but hers. "You think I found out about it and killed her, don't you?"

She felt like the worst sort of journalistic ghoul. "I'm sorry, Scott. I had to ask."

Scott struggled to pull himself together. When he spoke again, his voice was controlled, but it radiated fury. "I'll tell you one more time: there was nothing to find out. If there had been and if I'd found out about it, Frank Marquez would be the one being buried tomorrow, not Carrie."

Maybe she was overcompensating for her own feelings of guilt, but Amanda believed him. Admittedly, it helped that as soon as he left, the waitress confirmed that he had been in there the night that Carrie had been killed.

"I waited on him myself," she said, chewing on a wad of gum.

"Did you know the woman he was living with?"

"You mean the one who was killed?"

Amanda nodded.

"Sure, I did. She was in here a lot, sometimes with him, sometimes with that Cuban guy who runs the snack bar."

So Robert hadn't been lying, at least about Carrie's public friendliness with Frank Marquez. "Tell me about that. What was she like with the two of them?"

"She was obviously crazy about Scott. The two of them were like a couple of kids discovering puppy love. They'd just sit and stare at each other and hold hands."

"What about with the other man?"

"I don't know exactly. It always seemed pretty intense, like they were arguing about something."

"Like two ex-lovers?"

The waitress's mouth dropped open. "Are you kidding? Those two? No way. She was too much in love with the other guy, for one thing."

"Maybe that was the problem," Amanda suggested.

"Nah. I know human nature pretty well. You get to working in a dive like this. The stuff they talked about, it wasn't personal enough. Mostly business. Lately, it seemed like he was warning her about something and she wasn't listening. The last time he got so mad, he walked out and left her here."

"When was that?"

"A few days ago. Maybe two . . ." Her voice trailed off.

"Could it have been on the day Carrie was killed?"

She chewed her gum thoughtfully. "You know something, hon, I think it was."

CHAPTER
Six

After the waitress had walked away, Amanda just sat there, absentmindedly looking for any last crumbs of the cheesecake as she considered the addition of Frank Marquez to the list of suspects. What had he been warning Carrie about? Was it a sufficient motive for murdering her? If he was so angry, why hadn't she listened?

At this point it seemed that anything short of suicide was possible and equally likely. Robert or Jackson might have killed Carrie to keep her from revealing whatever she knew about the dual bookkeeping system. Alana Marquez, like Robert, might have suspected that Carrie was having an affair with her husband. And Scott—no matter how much she liked him, no matter how convinced she was of his innocence—could not be legitimately discounted as a suspect. Now that she really stopped to think about it, this coffee shop was close enough to Weights and Measures to make his alibi much weaker than it had seemed initially. That left her with at least five good suspects with possible motives and access to the murder scene. Terrific. Instead of eliminating suspects, she was adding them. In fact, unless someone generously confessed today, there was no way she could possibly unravel this story before the deadline Oscar had given her.

Steeling herself for battle, she took a quarter out of her wallet and went to the pay phone near the cash register to call the office. Her attempt to negotiate an extension of the deadline went about as well as the rest of her day.

Oscar said no.

She explained for what seemed like the millionth time that she was certain she and Donelli were onto something big, a story that was complex and titillating.

He repeated himself, a little less adamantly.

She hinted at an exclusive exposé of a major scam.

He gave her the weekend.

Since she did not normally work weekends, her appreciation was dimmed ever so slightly. She slammed the phone down.

Still fuming, she went back to Weights and Measures hoping to find that Donelli had finished plowing his fields and returned to detective work. He had. He was perched on a stool at the end of the snack bar. She should have found the sight reassuring. Instead, something about the arrangement set her teeth on edge.

It was just before the lunch crowd was due and Alana seemed to be taking advantage of the lull—and of Donelli's attention. She had her elbows propped on the counter. The top of her pink cotton uniform strained across her well-endowed chest. The expression on her face was rapt, as if she couldn't wait for the next Brooklyn-accented word to trip off Donelli's tongue. Amanda only barely resisted the urge to stop by and remind Donelli that he was supposed to be asking questions, not delivering a seductive monologue. He'd probably just tell her to stay out of his interrogation.

She found a seat at a table along the back wall and watched. It was an exercise in masochism and, added to last night's momentary panic, told her far more than she wanted to know about the depth of her feelings for Donelli. She'd been trying vainly for months now to convince herself that she wasn't hooked. That little twinge in the pit of her stomach as she watched him charm Alana said otherwise.

The man she assumed to be Frank Marquez was watching, too. Though he was taking clean glasses from an under-the-counter dishwasher, his eyes, dark as onyx, kept shifting toward Alana. His thin lips formed a grim slash across a pockmarked face. After casting one last sidelong glance at the engrossed couple, he came toward Amanda.

"You need a menu?"

"No." The cheesecake suddenly felt heavy in her stomach, but she couldn't very well take up space without ordering something. "I'll have the yogurt-and-fruit plate with a glass of iced herbal tea."

He went behind the counter and made up the order, but he couldn't keep his eyes off Alana and Donelli. Amanda couldn't tell if he was worried or angry. Quite possibly both. There was something hard and dangerous about Frank Marquez's expression that sent a chill down her spine and lifted him straight to the top of her list of suspects.

If Alana was aware of her effect on her husband, she paid no attention to it. When she poured another cup of tea for Donelli, she held it out so that he was forced to take it from her. Their fingers brushed. Amanda felt an unfamiliar knotting in her gut. She glanced at Frank and saw that her reaction was only a pale imitation of his. He looked like a man who'd just caught his wife in a compromising position and had no intention of letting the betrayal go unavenged. She actually shivered.

By the time Frank brought her fruit plate and tea, his features were more composed, though there was an unreadable glint in his eyes. Amanda set out to distract him before he decided to make mincemeat of Donelli or Alana or both.

"This looks wonderful. Where do you find such fresh fruit?"

He stared at her blankly, as if she'd questioned him in a foreign language. "What?"

"Where do you buy your produce?"

"The farmer's market," he said. "I am there when they open."

"Word must be out about the quality of the food here. You certainly have plenty of customers."

"Thank you. Yes. People know we serve only the best."

"You said we. Do you actually own the snack bar or is it part of the fitness club?"

"Alana and I, we own the business." There was a noticeable note of pride in his voice. His accent was thicker than Alana's, indicating that he might have arrived in the U.S. more recently, perhaps on the Mariel boatlift which brought thousands of Cuban refugees to the U.S. If that were true, his adaptation and business success would certainly be a source of pride. "We only rent the space from Robert and Jackson. If they expand, we will open a second snack bar."

That was a surprise. "I didn't know they were thinking of expanding."

There was a flash of uncertainty in his eyes. "I should say nothing. It is not for certain."

Based on what Robert had told her, it was more than uncertain. It was out of the question. They were simply keeping the club afloat long enough to sell it. She wondered how Frank would react to that news.

"You need anything else now, lady?"

"No, that'll be all," she told him. He returned to the counter, passing Alana on the way and pausing to say something that wiped the smile from her face. Moments later Donelli was paying his check. Amanda waited for him to join her, but instead he left through the gym. She stared after him in consternation.

Before she could follow him, though, Felicia Grant slid into the seat opposite her. She looked infinitely better than she had two nights before when she'd discovered Carrie Owens's body. There was color in her cheeks. Her makeup was flawless. Her exercise outfit was hot pink trimmed in turquoise, a daring choice for someone with her coloring. It worked. A matching headband held her auburn hair back from her face and coordinated socks had been pushed down her slender calves to gather at her ankles. That pear-cut diamond, large enough to buy an office building in Atlanta at today's prices, glittered on her left hand. Three gold bracelets adorned her right wrist. Yet another diamond nestled in the valley between her breasts. It appeared Trace Weston didn't stint when it came to handing out diamonds either. Amanda thought the jewelry was a little overdone for exercising. She couldn't begin to imagine what the woman put on to attend a party.

Felicia extracted a gold cigarette case out of her Gucci bag. She lit a cigarette with a matching gold lighter, took a long, slow drag, and then exhaled. She was the epitome of cool, rich sophistication . . . until you looked into her eyes. They were burning with a feverish intensity. This was a woman with a lot on her mind.

"I can't stop thinking about it," she said finally, grinding out the cigarette, then lighting another.

Amanda didn't pretend not to understand what she meant. "Murder is never easy to accept."

"You're a reporter, right? We talked the other night?"

"Yes."

"Are you working on a story about Carrie's death?"

"Actually I'm putting together a feature on the club's singles crowd. If I turn up anything on Carrie that fits in, I'll use it." It was true as far as it went.

"What have you found?"

"Nothing I'm prepared to discuss, just a lot of unsubstantiated rumors."

Felicia's control snapped. "Damn it, you have to tell me. The killer could be after me, too."

Amanda had to choose between reassurance and a vague possibility that would only terrify this already frightened woman. She went with reassurance. "I doubt it. You said you didn't see anyone near the sauna."

"And you believe me?" Felicia's stunning blue-green eyes, fringed with mascara-lengthened lashes, were wide with surprise and a hint of relief.

"Why not? Don't the police?"

She shook her head. "They think maybe I'm blocking it out. They want me to see a shrink, maybe get hypnotized."

"It's a long shot, but it could help."

"It could also put me in some serious danger. What would you do?"

Amanda recalled Donelli's histrionics over some of her choices and grinned ruefully. "I'm not the best person to ask. I'm used to taking certain risks."

"Then you'd do it?"

Amanda considered it thoughtfully, then nodded. "I'd do it."

"My fiancé's against it. He thinks it's crazy for me to get any more involved."

That fit with Weston's remarks this morning. He'd sounded very protective when he warned Amanda to keep Felicia's name out of the story. "It sounds like prudent advice, but what do you think? Deep down, when you're not worrying about your fiancé's reaction, when you're not scared?"

Felicia sighed. "I think it's something I've got to do. I didn't know Carrie all that well, but the image of her lying in that steam room is horrible. Maybe it'll go away, if I help them catch the killer."

"And maybe it won't," Amanda countered realistically.

"It doesn't matter. I have to do it." There was a sudden resolve in her eyes. "Thanks. You've helped."

Amanda made a spur-of-the-moment decision. "Felicia, if you want someone to come along, let me know. I'd be glad to do it."

"It'll make great copy, right?" she said with cynicism.

Amanda could not deny that was one reason she had made the offer. But there was also something about Felicia Grant that touched her. For all of her wealth and bravado, she seemed like a bewildered, lost girl, sad and a little lonely. Despite Trace Weston's generosity, the romance in her life must not be all that rewarding, if she was turning to a virtual stranger for advice. Or perhaps it was that crisis mentality that creates an instantaneous bond between victims of disaster.

"I'll come as a reporter or as your friend," Amanda said. "Your choice."

A faint smile touched Felicia's lips, then vanished. "Thanks. I'll let you know."

Then she left as abruptly as she'd appeared.

After that Amanda could not stop thinking about Felicia. Her appetite had been dulled by the conversation and by too much cheesecake, but still she sat, toying with the strawberries and chunks of pineapple and cantaloupe on her plate. She glanced up and saw that the snack bar was nearly filled to capacity. There was also a long line waiting for carry-out orders. She scanned the line with mild curiosity. Suddenly curiosity turned to something else, some vague sense that the pieces didn't fit. Perplexed, she studied the customers more closely.

When Donelli finally joined her, Amanda didn't even waste time questioning his absence. She nodded in the direction of the line. "Does anything about that strike you as odd?"

"You mean that so many people can stomach bean curd and this stringy stuff that passes for a vegetable?" He picked up a spare fork, poked around hopefully in her plate, then gave up in disgust. All he found amid the sprouts were chunks of fruit that had been repeatedly speared by her fork.

"I'm serious," Amanda said. "Look at them."

There were a few people still in their exercise clothes, some businessmen, a few well-dressed women obviously on their lunch hour. There were also several teenagers.

"What am I looking for?"

"Look at the number of teenagers. When you were that age, would you have come to a place like this for lunch?"

"Amanda, I supported at least three fast food franchises when I was a teenager. Who knows, though, maybe these kids grew up as vegetarians. There's a lot of that these days. People are into all this healthy stuff."

"Maybe," she said thoughtfully.

"What are you thinking, Amanda?"

"Do they look healthy to you?"

His gaze went back to the line. "No, they look . . ." His eyes widened. "Drugs?"

"Could it be that they're serving more than salads and juices in here?"

"Amanda, don't you think that's a pretty big leap in logic? Just because they look a little strung out, it doesn't mean they bought the stuff here."

"But it's possible, right?"

"Anything is possible," he admitted.

"And it could fit with something I heard earlier." She told him about Frank's argument with Carrie. "Maybe this is what she knew about."

Just then the first teenager in line picked up his order and started for the door. Amanda was on her feet at once. Donelli was two paces behind her. He grabbed her arm and spun her around.

"Where the hell are you going?"

"Where do you think? To talk to that kid."

"Oh no, you're not."

She pushed him back. "Will you just wait here," she hissed. "You might scare him off."

"Amanda! If you're right and Marquez killed Carrie because she stuck her nose in this, you'll wind up exactly like she did."

People were turning to stare at them. "Five minutes, Donelli. Please. Don't make me wish I'd left you working in those blasted fields. If Marquez comes after me or if I'm not back, you can dash to my rescue."

He glared at her, but he sat back down.

Outside, she caught up with the teen halfway down the block. She introduced herself and explained she was working on a story about Weights and Measures for *Inside Atlanta*. "Are you a member?"

The boy regarded her nervously and tried to ease past. She blocked his way.

"Nah," he said finally. "I just come here for lunch sometimes."

"You must like the food."

"It's okay."

"Any particular favorites?"

"Nah."

"Then why do you come? Are you a vegetarian?"

He stared at her blankly. Wherever he was, it was far from this street corner. Further questioning would be a waste of time.

"Never mind. Thanks for your time."

Two more interviews went much the same way before she decided her five minutes were up. Donelli would be hotfooting it through the door any minute. Back inside, she found him shredding a napkin. A satisfying look of relief swept over him when she appeared. On some level she didn't care to examine too closely, she liked the fact that he worried about her. Mack had accepted the idea that she could slay dragons all on her own and left her to it. She had basked in the respect for her strength, but there had been times when it left her feeling uncherished.

"Well?" he said.

"I don't know."

"What do you mean you don't know?"

"I couldn't very well ask the kids if they'd just bought drugs with their yogurt, for heaven's sake. But if I've ever seen a junkie, that first kid had all the symptoms. His eyes were all funny and he was shaking like a leaf. I'm not so sure about the other two. I'm going back outside."

This time Donelli didn't waste his breath. He picked up another napkin and began shredding it.

Amanda interviewed several more customers over the next hour, including a few of the businessmen and health club members as a diversion. She'd just come back to the table after the last one, when Frank Marquez appeared.

"What do you think you're doing, lady?"

Donelli rose slowly to his feet. He was taller and bulkier than Marquez, which compensated somewhat for the menacing expression in the Cuban's eyes.

"I beg your pardon?" Amanda said softly.

"Are you trying to ruin my business with all your questions? This is harassment. You ask and ask and soon no one will come back."

"I'm just working on that story about the singles crowd that hangs out at Weights and Measures. You know that. Robert and Jackson okayed it. I have to interview the members."

"Not everyone who comes here for my lunches is a member. They don't want to be bothered with a lot of questions. They're busy people. You're wasting their time."

"I haven't had any complaints. Most people think it's fun being interviewed for a magazine. They like seeing their name in print. It won't affect your business."

His dark eyes blazed with distrust, but he was apparently aware of Donelli's tense stance. He backed down. "You wrap it up soon or I complain to Roberto, you understand?''

''You've got it.'' She tapped her notebook. ''I have more than enough now.''

''I wish you hadn't said that,'' Donelli said in a low voice, when Marquez had walked away.

''Said what?''

''That you have more than enough. If Marquez is guilty of something, that line just might make him nervous.''

''Oh,'' she said and swallowed hard.

They left Donelli's battered old Chevy in town and drove to his house together. It gave her time to try to think of a way to uncover exactly what was going on in the Weights and Measures snack bar. They were nearly home when she had a brainstorm. She described her idea to Donelli. It involved Larry Carter, the photographer she'd worked with on the *Gazette*. He still worked there, but he also did free-lance work for *Inside Atlanta*.

However, the assignment she had in mind for him this time had nothing to do with photography. Larry had wheat-colored hair and freckles. He was in his early twenties, but he could definitely look younger.

''I don't know, Amanda,'' Donelli said with typical caution. ''It could be dangerous. The last time Larry got mixed up in one of your investigations, he ended up in the hospital. He may not be so keen on working with you again.''

"Who are you kidding? He said it was the most exciting thing that had ever happened to him."

"He said it while he was recovering from a concussion. I doubt that would hold up in a court of law."

"At least, let's talk to him about it. He can always say no."

"Amanda, men cannot say no to you. Your eyes go all misty and we immediately want to rush out and pull down the moon and hand it to you. Common sense flies out the window."

"You say no all the time."

"I've had practice. When I do, you'll notice that I'm staring at your chin. I cannot look you in the eyes and say it. Witness the fact that I left half a field unplowed today, so I could get into town to meet with Alana. Larry's just a babe in the woods when it comes to resisting your feminine wiles."

She frowned at him. "I do not indulge in feminine wiles," she said indignantly. "I'm just going to explain the situation and make a simple suggestion. If he's not interested, all he has to do is say so."

Donelli looked doubtful, but he finally nodded. "Call him, but I'm telling you, Amanda, if he has any qualms about getting involved, you are not to pressure him. We'll figure out an alternative plan."

"Promise," she said.

She did, however, stack the deck in her favor by inviting him to a doubleheader—the Braves against the Mets. The Atlanta Braves were Larry's only known vice, aside from an occasional beer. Amanda was almost convinced that he had chosen photography as a career simply because he could fit it in between games.

"The doubleheader's tomorrow night. Can you make it?" she inquired innocently.

"What's up?" he asked suspiciously.

"Nothing. Why would you ask that?"

"Because sitting in Fulton County Stadium at twilight when the temperature is ninety degrees is not usually your idea of fun. Before you got involved with Donelli, I asked you on at least forty-seven separate occasions to go to a game with me. You declined every time. I've never known a woman to wash her hair so much."

Amanda grinned. "Okay, so baseball is not my favorite sport."

"You don't have a favorite sport, unless it's typing."

"I like tennis."

"When was the last time you were on a court?"

"I watched Wimbledon last year. That ought to prove something."

"Of course it does," he soothed. "It was raining Fourth of July weekend."

"Larry, I am making a gesture here. Do you want to go to these damn games or not?"

"I'll go. I'll even spring for pizza afterwards," he offered. "Or does Donelli have you eating so much Italian food you'd rather go for Chinese?"

"I was thinking more on the order of alfalfa sprouts," she responded gleefully. "See you tomorrow."

"Alfalfa sprouts!" She cut off his incredulous shout before he could change his mind about going with her. She didn't think Larry considered any price too high for a chance to see the Braves, but she didn't want to press her luck.

"I take it he agreed," Donelli said, when she came back into the kitchen smiling. The smile faded.

She began setting the table, concentrating very hard on getting the silverware placed in precisely the right spot. Fork on the left, knife and spoon on the right, the ends aligned so evenly they could have been used to draw a straight line. She even got a paper towel to shine one of the spoons.

"Amanda? Did he agree or not?"

"Sort of," she mumbled.

Donelli stopped slicing the tomatoes and stared at her. "What does that mean?"

"Are those tomatoes from your garden? They look terrific. They're the biggest yet, right?"

"Don't change the subject," he said with the sort of single-minded purpose that had made him such a good cop. She rather regretted the fact that it had resurfaced at this particular instant.

"He agreed to go to the Braves' doubleheader tomorrow night," she said finally. "He doesn't know about my idea yet."

"When do you plan to tell him?"

"I thought I'd bring it up after the Braves score their first run."

"Good timing. What happens if it's a shut out?"

"Not even the Braves can be shut out for two consecutive games."

He picked up the sports section from the stack of papers on the floor by his back door. His finger tapped against a headline about the team's losing streak. "If I were you, I'd have a backup plan."

"I do."

"Oh?"

"I'm going to let you convince him it's his civic responsibility."

CHAPTER Seven

"Oh no, you don't,'' Donelli said adamantly. ''If you want to drag Larry into the middle of this, it's up to you to convince him. In fact, I'd love to hear your lecture on civic responsibility. I had no idea you'd become so dedicated to upholding the laws of Georgia.''

He was referring—rather nastily, she thought—to the break-in at Weights and Measures. He might also have meant her oft-stated disdain for the South in general and the rural area served by the *Gazette* specifically. He did not seem willing to credit her for the shift in her attitude since they'd met. Once she had gotten over her anger at Mack for stranding her hundreds of miles from the Metropolitan Museum of Art and Broadway, Amanda had begun to look at the small towns scattered between Atlanta and Athens with a more open-minded attitude. And, in fact, she was growing downright attached to the burgeoning culture and liveliness of Atlanta. She'd even come to enjoy the peace and quiet of her small country cottage after a lifetime of New York's frenetic energy.

"Donelli, my motives are pure," Amanda retorted with only the slightest twinge of guilt. "I'm always in favor of upholding any rational laws, especially those which punish murderers."

His lips twitched in amusement. "Amanda Roberts, you are motivated by your obsession with investigative journalism. You like the chase, the hunt, the intrigue. You can't stand dangling threads, any more than you can tolerate dangling participles. You are not dedicated to the salvation of the universe."

"That is not true! I'm not some sort of danger junkie. I only put my neck on the line to get at the facts, when I think it'll help to effect a change. You ought to understand that better than anyone."

"Why is that?"

If she had been paying better attention, she would have noticed that his voice was deceptively calm. That quiet tone almost always masked his rising fury. She blundered right along anyway. "Because despite this current lapse in judgment on your part, you are every bit as dedicated to the public good as I am. You hate lies and deceptions and crime."

"True, but that doesn't mean I think I'm the only person around who can cure the world's ills. There are a lot of excellent policemen out there, who're doing the job just fine."

"Maybe that's true. Maybe there's not a single crook

or murderer on the street because Joe Donelli's not on the job, but I don't give a damn about that. I care about you, about what you need."

"I have everything I need right here."

"That's bull, Donelli. This is no challenge for you. You've been running from challenges ever since you left New York. Why? What turned you into a quitter?"

Donelli's expression froze at the harsh label. She realized that in her effort to provoke him into telling her the truth behind his retreat to the country she had gone too far. Without another word, he turned back to the tomato on the counter. She heard the resounding *thwack* of the knife as it slammed through the tomato. Amanda winced. She had a sickening hunch he'd been imagining her neck under the blade of that knife.

"Joe," she said quietly. She saved the use of his first name for very special and usually intimate occasions. She hoped the use of it now conveyed the depth of her regret that their accusations had gotten out of hand.

He arranged the tomato slices on a plate so precisely that they could have been photographed for *Gourmet* magazine. He added rings of Vidalia onion and a sprinkle of salt and pepper with extraordinary precision.

"I'm sorry," she said, the apology swallowed up by the heavy silence. "I didn't mean to yell. It's just that I don't understand. I've watched you in action. I've known a lot of cops and I can tell you were a good one, probably one of the best. And I know the kind of man you are. You care. Was that it? Did you care too much?"

She moved up behind him and slid her arms around his waist. She rested her head against his back. His shoulders stiffened. ''Please,'' she pleaded. ''Talk to me.''

''Dinner's ready.''

He turned to put the plate of tomatoes on the table. Furious, she knocked it from his hand. Tomatoes and onions hit the floor and mingled with shards of china. ''Damn it, I don't care about dinner. I want to know what goes on in that head of yours.''

Methodically, he began cleaning up the mess. ''Save your questions for your next interview. My psyche's not open for discussion.''

Amanda knew then that it was pointless to argue any more tonight. She had approached the subject all wrong. Even so, she was hurt by his attitude, infuriated by his calm attempt to keep her at a distance. He was shutting her out, slamming doors so loudly the impact reverberated in her head.

''Then I guess I might as well leave,'' she said, grabbing her purse off the counter and bolting for the door.

All the way to the car, she listened for the screen door to open and for Donelli to call out. She heard nothing. The sound of silence spoke louder than any words he might have used.

The night was one of the longest and loneliest of Amanda's life. She'd been anticipating a confrontation with Donelli over his life-style for weeks, but she hadn't expected it to come last night. Nor had she expected it to end with her walking out. Running away from a problem was not her style, but Donelli had left her with very little choice. Unless he was willing to confide in her, they had no future. Perhaps it was time they both realized that.

After tossing and turning the entire night, she was ravenous. One of the most infuriating quirks of her personality was that stress made her hungry. Other people lost weight in a crisis. Amanda pacified herself with food.

She opened the door to the refrigerator and found a quart of sour milk and a stale loaf of bread. She had definitely been spending too much time at Donelli's. She got dressed and drove to the next town for breakfast at her favorite doughnut shop. Virginia Beatty served up gossip, humor and the best coffee in three counties. The pancakes weren't bad either—huge, light, and bursting with blueberries. Amanda placed a double order.

"What's on your mind, Amanda?" Virginia asked, lingering at her table after she'd poured a second cup of coffee.

"Nothing, why?"

"Because you only eat this much food when you've got troubles. Where's that sexy cop of yours?"

"Plowing a field, I suppose." She stuffed a huge bite of pancake into her mouth to avoid further comment.

"You two have a fight?"

She waved her fork in what she hoped was an evasive gesture.

"What about?" Virginia persisted.

She scowled up at her. "I came in here for breakfast. I did not come for counseling."

Virginia threw up her hands. "Fine. I was just trying to help."

Amanda sighed. "I know. I just don't feel like talking about it. At the moment, I want to forget Joe Donelli even exists."

"That might be hard."

"Not if I work at it," she said fervently.

"Well, start working, sugar, because the man is coming up the walk and he looks fit to be tied."

Before Amanda could identify a suitable escape route, Donelli was sliding into the booth, across from her. Virginia brought him a cup of coffee, then reluctantly left them alone.

"We need to talk," he said without preamble.

"How did you get here? Your car's in Atlanta."

"If you thought stranding me was going to get you out of this conversation, you don't know me very well. I hitched a ride to your place. When you weren't there, I hitched another ride here. Does that give you some idea of how committed I am to having this talk?"

"When I wanted to talk last night, you weren't in the mood."

"I'm still not in the mood, but I will not spend another night like last night. I can't even figure out what the hell you were so mad about. Why did you walk out? That's not your style."

"Which do you want to know first? Why I was mad or why I walked out?"

"Is there a difference?"

"I was mad because you're wasting your talent, you're

hiding behind this ridiculous farming thing. I left because you won't be open with me about the reason." She sighed deeply and pushed away the plate of half-eaten pancakes. "Joe, it scares me that you won't talk to me about the past. You know all about Mack and me. You know how much I hated moving down here, how unsatisfying my job was on the *Gazette*, how badly I wanted to move back north until I met you and came to terms with the past. You know what I like to eat, that I wear old socks around the house on chilly mornings. You even know whether or not I snore."

Donelli started to say something, but she stopped him. "Never mind. I'd just as soon not know about the snoring. If I do, I'd be afraid to fall asleep again. What I'm getting at is that there are times when I don't feel I know you at all. It's as though there's this black hole and great chunks of your past have fallen into it."

Donelli's expression was incredulous. "How can you say that, Amanda? You know just as much about me as I know about you. You know—to your everlasting regret—that I listen to country music. You know I used to be a cop. You've seen the scars from the knife wound I got in my chest and the bullet wound in my back. You know that I don't miss New York, that I like my little farm house, that I like the people down here. You know I like unbuttered toast for breakfast, that I prefer my eggs sunny-side up." He grinned at her. "And you know whether or not I snore. Why does it matter so damn much to you why I've made the choices I've made? I'm here now. You're here. Let's live in the present."

"I can't, not that easily."

"Why not?"

"Because whether you want to admit it or not, there is a very big part of you still living in the past. Be honest with yourself, if not with me."

He frowned at her. "I don't think this has anything to do with me or my needs, Amanda. It's you. You're the one who can't live with my being a simple farmer. You're embarrassed by what I do, isn't that it? There's no status, no prestige, no glamour. You're on a fast track and I'm content to stay at the station."

His cynical words slammed into her. "Do you honestly think that's what this is all about?"

"Isn't it?" he said stubbornly.

"Despite the ego massage provided by uniform groupies, Donelli, you and I both know that being a cop isn't all that glamorous, unless you're on 'Miami Vice.' It's your life. I'd be proud of you no matter what you did, if I thought you were fulfilled and happy."

"Then let me reassure you. I am fulfilled. I am happy."

"Then why do you seem more alive when you're dabbling in a murder case? Why do I sense your mind clicking as you sort through the clues? Why do your instincts seem sharper? Your eyes brighter? You don't look that way when you're talking about chinch bugs. You're a good detective, Donelli. You're wasting your potential. If you want to dabble, do it in your garden. Grow tomatoes and cucumbers and squash, if you want to, sell them at your roadside stand, but do it as a hobby. Put your energy into doing something meaningful."

"Farming is meaningful, Amanda."

"Of course it is, if you own a few thousand acres and provide food for the nation. You're treating it like a hobby. You take time away from it at the drop of a hat. You accuse me of not taking it seriously, but you don't treat it professionally yourself. If it is what you want, then prove it. Add more land, hire some men, and really turn your place into a farm. The vacation's over, Donelli. It's time to get back to work."

She wanted to kiss away his frown, but settled for touching his tightly clenched fist. "Just think about what I've said, okay?"

The frown remained, but he did say, "I think you're wrong, but okay. If it matters that much to you, I'll think about it. Just don't walk out on me again. I've gotten used to waking up with you beside me." He swallowed hard. "I don't want to lose you, Amanda."

Amanda met his gaze evenly. Her pulse fluttered, but she still managed to say with some conviction, "I won't walk out on a fight again, but I won't be staying at your place either. Not for a while, anyway."

"What are you saying?" he asked in a tight voice. "You want to break it off?"

"No, but I think we both need to do some serious thinking about whether we share the same values. The last few days have made that crystal clear."

"Do you honestly think that putting space between us is the way to resolve our problems?"

She sighed. "I'm not explaining this very well, but yes. When we're virtually living together, it's all too comfortable. It's too easy to ignore the underlying problems, to pretend they don't matter because everything else between us is so good."

"Maybe that's because they don't matter."

"If that's the case, then this is one way to find that out."

She left him to ponder that as she went to the pay phone and called Jenny Lee.

"What are your plans for tonight?" she asked. "Do you have a date?"

"Nothing I can't break if you want me to do some work for you."

Amanda outlined her plan. "I'm taking Larry to the Braves game tonight. I'm going to talk to him about it then. You want to come along? He's a nice guy. Maybe the two of you can work together on this. Two pairs of eyes will be better than one."

Jenny Lee was just about to respond when Donelli's low growl interrupted. "Amanda!" he warned.

"Gotta run, Jenny Lee. I'll be by to pick you up around four o'clock. Maybe you can have Shana stop by then. I'd still like to talk to her."

"I'll see what her plans are," Jenny Lee promised.

When Amanda had hung up, Donelli said, "Don't get that child mixed up in this."

"Don't let her hear you refer to her as a child. She's old enough to make her own decisions. It won't be dangerous. In fact, if she and Larry are in it together, they'll both be safer."

"I'm not sure how you figure that, but I suppose it's pointless to argue."

She grinned to hide her own concerns. "Yes."

"I'm still going with you today, Amanda."

"I thought we just agreed—"

"We agreed not to share my bed. That has nothing to do with the Carrie Owens investigation. You wanted me in on it. I'm in. Are we clear about that?"

Talk about being hoisted on your own petard, Amanda thought with a wry grin. "We're clear," she said reluctantly, sliding back into the booth. She automatically reached for her fork. She was suddenly starving again. She went to stab another chunk of blueberry pancakes, only to discover they were gone. Donelli looked guilty.

"Sorry," he said. "I thought you were through."

"I guess I was."

"By the way, you must be slipping. You never did ask me about that meeting I had with Alana yesterday."

"Well, what did she have to say?"

"Not much."

"Not much?" Amanda hooted. "Donelli, I saw the two of you. If the conversation had been any more engrossing, I'd have had to separate you with a hose."

"Crude, Amanda."

"But accurate."

"Okay, we talked, but I can't honestly say that anything significant came out of it. She met Frank shortly after he arrived on the Mariel boatlift. He came over from Cuba with one of her cousins and they called her family from

Key West as soon as they came ashore. After some long negotiations with Immigration and Naturalization, they were permitted to come to Atlanta.''

''What did she say about Frank? Anything about the state of their marriage?''

''She says Frank is very ambitious and that they won't always be running just a little snack bar like the one they have now. They're hoping for a chain.''

''Frank said something like that, too. He said if Weights and Measures expands its operation to another location, they'd open a second snack bar.''

''That's odd in light of what Robert said.''

''I thought so, too. What if he found out from Carrie that the club was up for sale?''

''So what? Why would that make him kill her?'' Donelli said. ''I like the affair angle better. Alana might be the jealous type, but I don't think she's a murderer. What if Carrie threatened to tell Alana about their affair? Would Frank be capable of killing her to stop her?''

''Capable? Absolutely. He got a very vicious look in his eyes when he was watching the two of you. I think he'd be capable of just about anything. What I don't understand, though, is why a man that possessive of his wife would want to have an affair in the first place.''

''Maybe it's just the macho mentality. It's accepted in some traditional Latin societies that men have mistresses. The women are expected to remain faithful.''

''Haven't they ever heard about the goose and gander and equal treatment under the law?''

"I think you're mixing up metaphors or something."

She glared at him. "You know what I mean."

"Hey, don't take it out on me. I didn't say I subscribed to the double standard, only that it exists."

"Never mind. Just finish your coffee. I want to go pick up Larry and Jenny Lee."

"Amazing."

"What?"

"You actually sound anxious to get to the ballpark."

"I am anxious to get moving on this case. In order to do that, if I have to put up with a few hours of suffering I will do it."

"Your sacrifice is duly noted. I'll mention it to Oscar."

"I doubt if he'll be impressed," she said dryly. "Especially when I put the tickets on my expense account."

"If I'd known you were going to do that, I'd have suggested we invite Alana and Frank, Robert and Jackson, maybe even Scott Cambridge. It would have been like one of those meetings Nero Wolfe has, when he gathers all the suspects in one place and reveals the murderer."

Amanda laughed. "There's only one tiny little drawback to turning tonight into that sort of confrontation."

"Oh?"

"Unless you know something I don't know, we don't know the identity of the murderer."

Donelli grinned back at her. "It's only two o'clock. Maybe you can figure it out before game time."

"I think we'd better just stick to the original cast for the evening—you and me, Jenny Lee and Larry."

"Don't you think Oscar'd like to be in on this one? You know how testy he gets when he's feeling left out. And after all, it is his money you're throwing around."

"If you want to be technical, it's *Inside Atlanta*'s, but you're probably right. I'll call him. Maybe he'll extend my deadline, once he hears about the drug angle. I didn't know about it when I talked to him yesterday."

"If he doesn't, does that mean you'll go back to covering something safe and boring on Monday?"

"No. It means I'll have to hide what I'm doing from Oscar."

He shook his head. "I knew it was too much to hope for. Come on, Amanda. Let's go hunt for clues."

"If I didn't know better, I'd actually believe you're enjoying this." The minute the words were out of her mouth, she regretted them. Why couldn't she learn to let well enough alone?

Donelli scowled and tossed some money down on the table for Virginia. "Don't press it, Amanda."

Before he could decide to dump the dregs of his coffee on her head just to make his point, Virginia interceded. "Amanda, honey, you have a call."

"Jenny Lee, no doubt."

"Nope. It's a man."

She sighed. "Then it must be Oscar. The man has the tracking skills of a bloodhound."

Virginia shook her head. "I don't think so. I'd have recognized the voice."

Curious, Amanda went behind the counter and picked

up the receiver that Virginia had left laying on top of the neat little rows of cereal boxes.

"Yes, this is Amanda Roberts."

"Drop the Carrie Owens story." The order was blunt, unadorned and terrifying. The voice was muffled and distorted, and unrecognizable. The only thing Amanda could be certain of was the menace. It wasn't the first time in her life she'd received a threatening phone call, but it was impossible to get used to the chill such a call sent down her spine. This one was particularly unnerving because the person had found her here, had obviously been watching her. Cold sweat broke out on her forehead.

"Who is this?" she demanded, trying to keep her voice steady. Even so, it rose enough to alert Donelli, who'd been standing at the end of the counter joking with Virginia. He moved in and tried to grab the phone from her hand, but Amanda held tight.

"Just do what I tell you, lady. Drop the story."

"Why should I?" she said, trying to pin down what it was about the voice that she recognized. *Lady*. He had called her that, just the way Frank Marquez had several times. She listened for some hint of a Cuban accent.

"Because you won't like the alternative."

The accent wasn't there, but her palms were sweating, her voice shaky when she replied, "Which is?"

"You'll die . . . just the way she did."

CHAPTER

Eight

Amanda tried to get her breath. The image of Carrie Owens sprawled ungracefully on the white tile floor of the steam room surfaced to taunt her. She whirled around and ran outside with Donelli right behind her. This time she couldn't seem to get away from the memory of Carrie's death stare. She knew somehow that if she closed her eyes, even for an instant, the face in her mind would change and become her own.

"Who was that on the phone? What's wrong?" Donelli demanded as she leaned against the car and drew in great gulps of air.

"Can't breathe," she responded in a choked voice, her heart hammering in her chest, blood roaring in her ears. She'd heard the note of alarm in his voice, but was incapable of reassuring him.

His arms slid around her. Hard and real and comforting. Right now, she needed to feel surrounded by that instinctive, unquestioning protectiveness. Her own weakness wouldn't last. She would chafe again at his bossy interference, but for now she was grateful for his strength.

"Take it easy," he murmured soothingly, ignoring his own panic to calm hers. "You're okay. I'm here. You're just fine. Take a nice, slow breath."

Finally, her pulse began a more even rhythm. With a shuddering sigh of relief, she rested her head against Donelli's shoulder, listened to the steady beat of his heart. "Sorry."

"Don't be sorry." He stepped back a pace, but didn't release her from the reassuring circle of his arms. "Feeling better?"

She realized then that Virginia had followed them to the street and was looking on anxiously. "You okay, hon?" she asked. "I could bring you a cup of tea, if you don't want to come back inside."

"Thanks, Virginia. I'm okay. Sorry for the uproar."

"Stop apologizing," Donelli ordered, when Virginia had left them alone. "Let's get in the car and I'll take you home."

She heard the overprotective note in his voice. It meant he planned to play the white knight, to fill up the moat and pull up the drawbridge to keep her safely out of harm's way. She loved him for wanting to, but she could not allow it. It was time to draw on her own inner resources again.

"Forget it," she told him firmly. "Nothing's changed. We're going to get Jenny Lee and Larry."

He shook his head. His jaw tensed and his lips set stubbornly. "You forget it, Amanda. You're too upset."

"It's not a terminal condition. The call just threw me for a minute, that's all. I've been through worse."

"That doesn't mean you have to tough it out."

"Yes, it does. Don't you see? I can't let the killer think I've been scared off."

"Then blame it on me. I'm scared off. If you could have seen your face . . ." He shuddered. "My God, Amanda, you looked like you'd heard from a ghost. What makes you think the call was from the killer?"

"It was either him or someone with a stake in seeing that the case goes unsolved."

"It was a man's voice?"

"Absolutely. Even though it was muffled, it sounded too deep to be a woman's."

"What did he say?"

"Just the usual stuff," she evaded.

"And what *stuff* is that?"

She tried to be nonchalant. "That if I didn't drop the story, I'd end up like Carrie Owens."

Donelli turned deathly pale and threw up his hands. He had obviously guessed it was something like that, but hearing her confirm it made him a little crazy. "Terrific! That's just great! Someone threatens to kill you, unless you get your nose out of this case and you plan to ignore them. What's it going to take, Amanda? A bullet through your heart?"

She shivered, despite her conviction that he was overreacting. "Donelli, I'm not going to do anything stupid like wander down a deserted alley after dark. But I'm also not going to go into hiding. I refuse to live my life that way again. That month in New York after the car bomb, when the only companions I had were vice cops, was the worst time in my life. I won't be shut away like that again."

"Amanda—"

She kissed him gently to shut him up. "Don't. I have to do my job."

He studied her implacable expression and relented finally. "Then we go back to my place for my gun. And another thing, I'm not letting you out of my sight until this is over with. All that stuff about space will just have to wait until this is over. No arguments, okay?"

That would be too easy. A part of her wanted him within sight, within reach, especially in the dark hours before dawn. She drew in a deep breath and said, "No."

"Amanda, the subject is not open for discussion."

Her chin rose a fraction. "No," she agreed. "It's not."

Eyes that glinted like just-fired steel challenged her. Her own gaze didn't waver. Finally, Donelli sighed.

"We'll talk about it tonight."

"A few hours won't change my mind."

"Tonight, Amanda."

She managed a faltering grin. "You are one stubborn SOB, Donelli."

He grinned back. "Takes one to know one, Amanda."

The one thing Amanda didn't argue about was the gun. There would have been no point to it, since Donelli had made up his mind. She would use her capitulation on that as a bargaining point later. Besides, the idea of having it nearby, in the possession of a man with Donelli's skill was definitely reassuring.

After they'd gotten the gun and he had decided she could be safely left alone to pack a few things while he made a phone call to Oscar, and after he'd checked every door and window lock on her cottage, they went to pick up Jenny Lee.

When they arrived, Shana was sitting in the living room, a dark-haired little boy in her lap pointing at pictures in a magazine. As she identified each object, he repeated the word, his face screwed up in concentration. Her total absorption gave Amanda a few minutes to study her.

Shana was in her midtwenties with dark brown hair cut short to wisp around a serious, round face that had a sort of wholesome beauty about it. She was dressed in shorts, a baggy T-shirt, and sandals. Her legs were tanned and long enough for Donelli to admire in a way that made Amanda envious.

"Jenny Lee tells me you knew Carrie," she said finally.

Shana looked up and nodded. "I wouldn't say we were close friends, but yes, I knew her as well as anyone else at the club did, aside from Scott."

"How do you feel about taking over her classes?"

"I'm glad to do it temporarily, but with this little guy," she ruffled his hair, drawing an angelic smile, "I don't want to give up my evenings for too long. I told Robert and Jackson that."

"Wasn't there anyone else at the club who wanted those classes?"

"Not really. One of the girls can substitute in aerobics in a pinch, but for the most part the others work best with the equipment. Only Carrie and I had aerobics experience. She worked at some fancy spa for a while before she came here."

"Here in town?"

"No. I think it was in California."

"Why did she leave? I mean that sounds like the perfect position for someone in your business."

"She never really said, but I got the feeling she followed some man here. Whoever it was, it was over before she came to work at Weights and Measures. She and Scott really had a good thing going. She adored him, even though she worried sometimes about the age difference."

"What's the story about her and Frank Marquez?"

The question drew the same blank stare it had at first from Scott. "As far as I know, there is no story. I think they were friendly. They took breaks together occasionally, especially the last couple of weeks, but that was it."

"How long have you been at the club?" Amanda asked.

"Four years. I was there when Robert and Jackson came on."

"Any problems with the transition?"

"Not for me. They've been good for the place. We're busier than ever. Robert's always on the make, but he's not obnoxious about it. If you turn him down, he gives up. He did with me, anyway, and I think it was that way with Carrie, too."

"Jenny Lee mentioned that you thought Carrie was upset the last week or so. Any idea at all what was on her mind?"

"Not really. I asked her a couple of times if she wanted to talk about what was bothering her, but all she said was that she had some decisions to make. I don't even know if they were professional or personal."

Amanda was at a loss. She looked at Donelli and caught him making faces at Shana's son. The child was giggling and struggling to get down from his mother's lap. He toddled straight over to Donelli and held up his arms. A warm, unfamiliar sensation swept through Amanda as she watched him pick up the boy. He was bouncing him on his knee when she finally interrupted to ask, "Anything I missed?"

Donelli might have appeared distracted, but he had apparently heard the entire interview, because he didn't hesitate. "It's an obvious question and I'm sure the police asked you this, too, but do you have any idea who might have hated Carrie enough to kill her? Did Scott have an old girlfriend who was jealous, maybe? Was there anyone who hung out around the club watching her? Anything at all?"

"Sorry. I can't really say. Scott's last relationship broke up months before Carrie came on the scene. As for the other, our shifts only overlapped by a couple of hours. If there was anyone watching her, I never saw him."

Amanda sighed. They'd learned virtually nothing new except that Carrie had worked in a California spa before coming east. It was not exactly a productive interview. "Thanks, Shana. I appreciate your seeing us."

"No problem," she said, picking up her son and going to the door. Amanda walked with her. "I hope they catch the person who did it soon. Some of the other girls are getting nervous.''

''Why?''

''They're afraid it'll turn out to be one of those weirdo serial killers.''

When she'd closed the door behind Shana, Amanda looked back at Jenny Lee and Donelli. Jenny Lee was looking pale, Donelli thoughtful.

''Now come on, you two. You don't really think we're dealing with a serial killer, do you?''

''It's a possibility we ought to consider,'' Donelli said. ''We've been assuming all along that the killer was only after Carrie. We don't really know that's the case.''

''I think it was,'' Amanda said with conviction. ''I think Carrie knew something and was threatening to talk. If we can figure out what it was she knew, I think it'll lead us straight to the killer. That's why we have to go ahead with this drug angle. We have to convince Larry to help us.''

''That's fine, but I'm more convinced than ever that Jenny Lee shouldn't get involved. We might just be setting her up as another target.''

''I'm willing to do it,'' Jenny Lee said, tilting her chin stubbornly. ''Amanda would.''

Donelli shot a rueful glance at Amanda. ''I don't consider that a sterling recommendation.''

Amanda grinned at him. ''Give it up, Donelli.''

He shrugged and led the way to the car. Twenty minutes later they had picked up Larry and were on their way to Fulton County Stadium.

Sitting in the backseat, Jenny Lee took one long look

at Larry, resplendent in shorts, running shoes, and his favorite Braves T-shirt and cap. She swallowed hard and fell silent. Amanda recognized the awed expression. It was the same one she'd worn for the first two years of her marriage to Mack. Larry seemed pleasantly oblivious to the instantaneous adoration. In fact, he seemed intent on treating Jenny Lee like a kid sister who was interfering with his date.

"Amanda tells me you're a photographer," Jenny Lee said.

Larry pulled his glance away from Amanda long enough to nod at her. "Yeah. Hey, Amanda, what kind of seats did you get?"

"They're in the stadium. How should I know what kind of seats they are?"

"Didn't you ask? They could be out in center field or something."

"Not the way the Braves are playing," Jenny Lee said. "We'll probably have the whole place to ourselves."

Larry scowled at her. "They're in a slump, that's all. They'll pull out of it." He turned back to Amanda. "What's this all about anyway? You still haven't explained."

"Let's wait."

"For what?"

"Oscar's coming, too," Jenny Lee explained.

Larry's mouth fell open. "You talked Oscar into coming to a ball game?"

"Actually, Donelli talked him into it," Amanda said.

Larry sat back, his expression bemused.

"How did you get interested in photography?" Jenny Lee asked. Larry stared at her blankly. "Photography," she prompted. "Did you study it in school?"

"Yeah. Amanda, does this have anything to do with that fitness club story you've been doing? I saw in the paper that some instructor was murdered at one of the clubs."

Before Amanda could answer, Jenny Lee said, "Yes. Amanda and I were there the night it happened."

Larry's gaze never wavered from Amanda. "You didn't tell me that."

Jenny Lee seemed to be gnashing her teeth. Fortunately, they arrived at the stadium just then. While Donelli and Larry went to pick up the tickets, Jenny Lee turned her furious gaze on Amanda. "That man!" she huffed.

"Larry?"

"Of course, Larry. What's the matter with him? He acts as if I don't even exist. How am I supposed to work with someone like that? You'd think I was ten and he was middle-aged or something."

"It's nothing personal," Amanda soothed. "Larry treats all women like pals. He's just an overgrown kid himself."

"Kid, hell. He's an insulting, overbearing, cocky boor, who thinks he's too good for a mere receptionist."

"Where on earth would you get an idea like that? Larry doesn't have an egotistical bone in his body."

"Amanda, you're the only person in the car he even knew existed. Donelli and I might as well have been on another planet. This is not the first time he's reacted like that around me. He comes into the magazine sometimes and looks straight through me to check out the newsroom to see if you or Oscar are around. You know I'm telling the truth. He didn't even recognize me tonight. If you ask me, he's insufferable and rude."

Finding amusement in the sparks flying between two of her favorite people was one thing. Seeing her scheme go up in smoke was quite another. "Jenny Lee, for heaven's sake, don't say that to him. I want you to work with the man, not date him. He's a damn good photographer."

"This assignment doesn't require his photographic skills. It requires acting skills. We're supposed to be a couple. He can't drag me into that place after drugs if he's going to treat me like a mentally deficient ten-year-old."

"He doesn't even know about the assignment. Give me a chance to explain it to him. I guarantee you he'll pull through."

Jenny Lee looked doubtful. "Okay, but don't blame me if I wring his neck before we're done."

"After you're done," Amanda cautioned. "Please."

Jenny Lee grinned. "Fine. After we're finished. It'll give me something to look forward to."

Donelli and Larry returned with Oscar in tow. They found their seats, then fortified themselves with hot dogs, popcorn, and beer. By the time the first pitch was thrown, Larry had resettled his Braves cap on his head at a more rakish angle at least a dozen times. Donelli was scanning the stadium with the practiced eye of a cop, apparently expecting Carrie's murderer to turn up with a more direct warning. Oscar was grumbling because Amanda wouldn't reveal what they were doing there.

"In good time, Oscar. All in good time."

"Amanda, it's hotter than hell out here. You said this was important. You dragged me away from home on a Saturday night. My wife's furious because I'm missing my son's birthday party at the country club."

"Oscar, you know perfectly well you hate the country club because they make you wear a coat and tie. You should be grateful to me."

"Okay, so I wasn't crazy about the idea of getting all duded up just to sit around with a bunch of Harriet's hoity-toity friends. That doesn't mean that missing it is worth the grief I'll get at home."

"You said you wanted to be kept up-to-date on the Carrie Owens story."

"You could have done that on the phone."

Already on edge, she finally lost patience. "Oscar, chill out, would you please?"

The snap in her voice drew Larry's attention. "Okay, Amanda, you might as well spill it. Even I can figure out that this isn't a social outing. The only one here who actually wants to watch baseball is me."

"And me," Jenny Lee piped in adamantly. Larry looked at her, really looked at her, for the first time.

"You like the Braves?" he said.

"If you'd been listening in the car, you'd have known that. Despite the lousy way they've been playing, they are second only to the Chicago Cubs in my heart."

Larry looked wounded. But as Jenny Lee began reciting statistics in support of her contention that the Cubs were worthy of her admiration, his expression grew thoughtful, then increasingly intrigued. Now Amanda was less worried about them killing each other than she was about getting their attention long enough to plot the sting operation at Weights and Measures.

Donelli shot her an understanding grin. Oscar had given up on getting information out of her and had gone to get another beer.

"Seems to me your plan may be working out too well," Donelli leaned down to whisper in her ear. She smiled ruefully.

"I know. And to think that an hour ago, she was vowing to wring his neck."

When Oscar got back with his beer, she interrupted Larry and Jenny Lee. "Okay, let's talk about my reason for getting you all together."

Quickly, she outlined what she and Donelli suspected about drugs being sold at Weights and Measures. "We have no way of knowing for sure who's behind it, if it's connected in any way to Carrie Owens's death or, for that matter, if it's even happening."

She looked at Larry and Jenny Lee. "That's where the two of you come in. My guess is that most of the sales are to teenagers. I want you to start hanging around the snack bar, talk to some of the teens, see what you can find out."

Oscar and Larry both started talking at once. Oscar was the loudest, so she let him go first.

"Turn the information over to the police, Amanda. I'm all for investigative reporting, but you need someone official behind you before you do something like this."

"I have someone official behind me. You. *Inside Atlanta* has every right to follow up on whatever leads it gets. Of course, I'll turn over whatever I find, but right now all I'm dealing with is speculation."

"Amanda, it's too dangerous. Drugs are big business and when you start threatening someone's income, they're liable to get really nasty." He turned to Donelli. "What do you think?"

Donelli shrugged noncommittally. "You know how much attention she pays to me."

"I still want an objective opinion. How much danger will these two be walking into?"

"It's hard to say, but if Carrie Owens did find out about a drug operation, then I think that speaks for itself."

"I don't like it," Larry said. Amanda's heart sank. She'd expected him to be anxious to get involved. She'd counted on his enthusiasm overriding Donelli's and Oscar's caution. She hadn't counted on having Jenny Lee bring all his masculine protectiveness surging into play.

"You can't ask Jenny Lee here to get mixed up in something like this," he said, casting a worried glance in her direction. "She's just a—"

Jenny Lee's face took on a mutinous expression. "Lawrence Carter, I am twenty-two years old. I am not a kid, nor am I an imbecile. If you can do this, so can I."

Larry appeared thunderstruck by the outburst. From the expression on Donelli's face, she had a hunch he sympathized with him.

"Larry, it won't be a problem," she reassured. "Jenny Lee's already a member of the club. It'll be perfectly natural for her to bring in another friend. They won't suspect her."

"They suspect you, don't they?"

"What makes you say that?" she said cautiously.

"Donelli told me about the call you got earlier. The threat."

"What threat?" Oscar demanded. His eyes narrowed. "You didn't say anything to me about a threat. Damn it, Amanda, I'm going to assign you to write gardening tips, if you're not careful. Maybe then you'll stay out of trouble."

"I'll quit and you know it, so let's cut all the nonsense." She glared at Larry. "I don't see what you're all worked up over. It was just a phone call."

Larry and Donelli exchanged a commiserating glance. "Amanda, somebody knows you're an investigative reporter for *Inside Atlanta*, they know you'd rather dig for news than write some piece of fluff, and they obviously suspect that you're going to learn something they don't want in print," Donelli reminded her with astonishing patience. "If you're in danger, then so is anyone who might be connected with you on this story."

"It's a risk I'm willing to take," Larry said. "But forget about Jenny Lee."

"I'll speak for myself," Jenny Lee retorted. "Count me in, Amanda. If he doesn't want to work with me, I'll do it by myself."

"You will not," Larry thundered so furiously that he didn't even notice when the Mets went ahead by two on an off-the-wall double. It was probably just as well. It would have just made an already bad evening worse.

Donelli jumped in. "Why don't we all take the weekend to think about this? We can talk it out on Monday. That's the soonest we can do anything, anyway."

Reluctantly, Amanda agreed.

By Monday nothing had changed. If anything, everyone was even more entrenched in his or her position. Donelli was growling because he'd spent two nights sleeping in his car on Amanda's front lawn after she stuck to her word about not letting him in the house. Oscar was ready to call Detective Harrison, Larry wanted to work alone, and Jenny Lee was stubbornly insisting that he would either take her along or she'd investigate things on her own. Amanda felt a little like a playwright who had assembled a cast of characters, only to have them write their own scripts.

Oscar finally agreed to hold off making the call to the police for another twenty-four hours. Jenny Lee stormed off to tackle the assignment on her own. Grumbling under his breath, Larry followed her. Amanda watched them enviously.

Apparently Donelli guessed her thoughts. "You stay away from Weights and Measures tonight," he said. "Let Larry and Jenny Lee snoop around and drive back out here with whatever information they come up with."

"But they might need backup."

"And you'll be a wonderful help to them, won't you?"

"Don't be sarcastic, Donelli. I know how to fire a gun."

"But you don't own one."

"No, but you do."

"Forget it. You're not going. I'm not going. And my gun is staying right where it is."

"Which is?" She tried to slide the question in so he wouldn't notice it.

He grinned tolerantly. "Out of harm's way."

"Sometimes you carry this protective streak of yours just a little too far. And, if you say one word about it being for my own good, I will personally yank every one of your tomato plants from the ground."

She stomped from the room, slamming the screen door emphatically behind her.

As soon as Donelli went to the store to pick up the ingredients for lasagna, she headed for Atlanta.

It was too bad about the lasagna, she thought as the speedometer hit sixty, then sixty-five. It was one of the best meals in Donelli's extensive repertoire of Italian recipes. Then, again, she still might get to taste it. In fact, Donelli might very well stuff it down her throat when he discovered that she had skipped out on him.

CHAPTER
Nine

A*manda* stopped in the nearly deserted locker room to change clothes, then strolled ever so casually through the gym until she found the perfect spot from which to keep an eye on the snack bar. Unfortunately, it was where the exercise bikes were located. Reluctantly, she climbed on and began pedaling as she watched for the arrival of Larry and Jenny Lee.

After nearly half an hour of riding, her thighs were cramping and her knees were like jelly, even though she kept the blasted bike on the lowest possible tension. She was also growing increasingly anxious. What on earth had happened? Were they standing on a corner somewhere battling about their plan? Or was Larry still trying to talk Jenny Lee out of coming?

"Hello, Amanda."

Jackson's softly spoken greeting caught her by surprise. She hadn't expected him to be here at this hour. Had he been watching her, anticipating her return, waiting for her?

The skin on the back of her neck prickled in alarm as she considered the possibility that he might be the one who had called and threatened her. Her shoulders stiffened and her grip on the handlebars tightened.

She turned reluctantly to find him standing right behind her, an enigmatic expression on his face. Since she couldn't seem to squeak a word past the sudden tightness in her throat, she settled for smiling. The only positive note she could find in his arrival was that she was able to stop pedaling.

"I'm surprised to see you here at this hour," he said. Was there an ominous note in his voice or was it merely her imagination working overtime?

"It's only eight-thirty." She didn't dare ask him about his presence. He owned the place. He could be here at three in the morning if it suited him,

He glanced at the clock. "Even so, most of our singles have left by now."

She nodded. "I know. I'm not really working tonight. I'm just doing my exercise routine."

"Overdoing it, actually. You're only supposed to spend fifteen to twenty minutes on the bike. I saw you when you came in. You've been at it for at least thirty minutes."

"Have I?" she said. Her startled reaction wasn't feigned. It had felt more like a full hour. "I guess I lost track of the time. I'll move on as soon as I finish this last mile."

Jackson nodded. "Okay. Just ask if you need any more instruction about your routine."

She heaved a sigh of relief as he wandered away. She

reflected that her nerves must be in bad shape for such a seemingly innocuous encounter to throw her so much. Still, it was odd for him to take such a personal interest in a member's exercise, just as it was unusual for him to be around at night. Before she could begin worrying anew about the implications of his concern, she glimpsed Larry finally coming through the door. The last thing she wanted to do was arouse Jackson's suspicions any further by staying on the bike after he'd already warned her she was overdoing it.

She decided she might be able to keep a watch on things by doing a few floor exercises in front of the floor-to-ceiling mirror. She could observe what was happening in the snack bar by checking out the reflection in the mirror.

Larry was wearing his faded jeans and his well-worn Atlanta Braves T-shirt. With his blond hair tousled, he appeared not much older than a teenager. There was no sign of Jenny Lee, but to complete his cover, he'd apparently struck up a conversation with a teen customer outside. The two of them were talking like old buddies as they approached the counter. No one would suspect they weren't just a couple of kids grabbing a late bite to eat.

She hoped.

Jenny Lee came in a few minutes later and settled on a stool at the far end of the counter. Larry didn't appear startled by her arrival, so apparently the two of them had settled on a plan. He drew her into his conversation with the other teen and Jenny Lee joined them in the take-out line.

Amanda would have given anything to know what they

were talking about. She held what remained of her breath as she watched to see what Frank Marquez was doing. Initially he regarded Larry warily, but it was obvious he knew the other young man and he was reasonably friendly to Jenny Lee. Eventually, he nodded, scribbled their order on his pad and went to assemble it.

Frank filled three plastic containers with salad, then toasted some pita bread and wrapped it in foil. He added two bottles of apple juice and one of sparkling water. Amanda grinned at the pained expression on Larry's face. He preferred a soft drink with his breakfast and lunch, and beer with his dinner. Wine was reserved for special occasions. Apple juice was not on his menu. Water—sparkling or otherwise—was meant for doing laundry.

Frank reached for a white take-out bag. When he placed the order inside, he added napkins, forks, and packets of sugar before ringing the sale up on the register. Something about the transaction troubled Amanda, but she couldn't quite put her finger on it. To all appearances, it had been a typical take-out dinner order. Had Larry decided to play it cautiously on this first encounter? Maybe he wanted to gain Frank's confidence before attempting to buy whatever illegal substances the man was selling.

Something continued to nag at her as she watched Larry, Jenny Lee, and the teen leave the snack bar. She was on her way to the showers when it struck her—the sugar packets. They were the false note. None of the trio had ordered coffee or tea or anything else requiring sugar.

Was it possible that the sugar packets contained drugs? Was there more than one box of sugar packets behind the counter? That had to be it. She could hardly wait to meet Larry to discover if she was right. She was less enthusiastic about seeing Donelli. He took a dim view of discoveries she made by risking her neck.

Of course, tonight there had been very little risk, she rationalized. No one could possibly have suspected that she was at the club for anything more than her regular routine. Not even Jackson. In retrospect, she thought she'd handled the conversation with him with reasonable aplomb. Of course, now she would probably have to ride the stupid bike for thirty minutes every night, since she had pretended it was such a breeze.

She hurried into the locker room to grab her purse, hoping she could catch up with Larry and Jenny Lee before they left for her house. She wouldn't mind having an escort for her arrival. It might postpone Donelli's explosion.

There were only two other women lingering by the sinks, repairing their makeup before facing the world. Amanda heard their exchange of good nights as she began working the combination number on her locker. A shower was running in the background. She heard the door to the locker room swing open, then nothing, not even the faintest rustle of movement. She glanced down the row of lockers and saw no one. Perhaps whoever it was had changed her mind. She shrugged and reached for her purse, but a sudden intimation of danger made her hesitate, straining to hear some hint of stealthy movement. The warm, thick air in the locker room seemed to vibrate with negative energy. Her pulse raced, then slowed as she tried to convince herself nothing was amiss.

That was the moment the big, wraparound towel dropped over her head. Its thick, absorbent material shut out the light and, worse, cut down her oxygen supply. She started to scream, but a hand held the terry cloth tightly over her mouth and nose. Her lungs fought for air, the effort painful and futile.

The memory of Carrie lying in the steam room, smothered to death, gave her a renewed surge of strength. Recalling the telephoned threat only two days before, she panicked. She struggled, tearing at the towel, kicking out at the unseen attacker. Some blows actually hit their target, but the person was larger and stronger than she. Whoever it was also had the advantage of surprise on his or her side. She cursed her stupidity in letting down her guard for even a single minute. Donelli was going to be furious.

She tried to draw in a deep breath, but it was as if the room were suddenly airless. Finally, with a last ragged gasp, she fainted.

Donelli was kissing her. She'd recognize the tender persuasiveness of those lips under any circumstances. In spite of feeling incredibly weak, Amanda found herself responding. She drifted pleasantly back to earth from some dreamless place. Her eyes blinked open, then closed against the glare of bright lights. She smiled.

"Hi," she said, surprised to discover that her throat felt sore, the way it sometimes did when she'd yelled too loudly and too often at some belligerent source who would not cough up public information.

Donelli closed his eyes and breathed a sigh of relief. "Thank God," he whispered, holding her close and rocking her.

Puzzled, she put a hand on his cheek and felt dampness. He had been crying. Donelli, her tough, courageous, battle-scarred ex-cop, had been crying. It didn't make sense. Nor did the low murmur of voices. They usually didn't kiss with an audience.

"What's wrong?" she asked, struggling to bring the picture into focus.

"You weren't breathing, that's what's wrong. You scared the hell out of me."

Her mind seemed to be trapped in some sort of dense fog in which answers lay tantalizingly out of reach. She couldn't quite grasp why he was so furious now, when just a minute ago he'd been kissing her so passionately.

Or had he been kissing her?

"You weren't kissing me, were you?"

His brown eyes blinked wide. "Kissing you? No, damn it, I was trying to save your life, the one you don't seem to give a damn about."

"Oh," she said meekly as the evening's events came flooding back. She heard the club staff moving the crowd back to give her more air. And she suddenly regretted the untimely lifting of the fog. Donelli might have been less likely to explode if she were suffering from amnesia. Then again, he seemed determined to remind her of the stupidity of her behavior.

"I thought I told you to stay put this afternoon, but do you listen? Oh, no. Instead, you come barreling back over here and nearly get yourself killed. I swear to God, Amanda, I'm going to chain you down the next time you get mixed up in one of your big stories."

She consoled herself with his apparent acknowledgment that there would always be a next time. It was progress of a sort. She waited until the tirade wound down before inquiring, "What exactly happened?"

"You're asking me? How the hell should I know? You were here. I wasn't."

"You're yelling."

"I am not yelling!" he shouted.

"Oh, really?"

He looked chagrined. "Sorry." His arms tightened around her. "Damn it, Amanda, why do you insist on doing stuff like this?"

"Donelli, it's okay. I'm going to be fine."

"That's not the point. This time you were lucky. And the last time. And the time before that. How many chances do you think one person gets?"

"You got a few yourself when you were a cop."

"I know, but I knew when to quit."

"You didn't quit because you were scared, Donelli. That's the one thing I'm certain of, despite your refusal to tell me anything. And it still bothers you that you're no longer in an official position to make a difference."

"And you are? You think this story is so important? World peace is important, Amanda. World hunger is important. This . . . this is a few pages in a monthly publication in Georgia, a fleeting damn ego trip."

Infuriated, she struggled out of his embrace and glared

at him. "And what if it means an end to a drug operation, is that important? What if it exposes somebody who's preying on kids, ruining their lives, is that important? It may not be as earth-shattering as achieving world peace or ending world hunger, but I'm damn proud of what I do."

Her speech took what little energy she had. Reluctantly, she sank back in Donelli's arms. Since he didn't drop her, she decided he couldn't be too furious.

He sighed. "I know that. And deep down, I guess I'm proud that you stick with it, but sometimes . . ."

"Sometimes what?" she said softly, sensing that they were getting close to an important truth.

"Sometimes I get terrified for you . . . and for me. I don't think I could bear it if some creep killed you."

"If you were a cop again, you could help me get the creeps off the streets. I'm not the only one they're hurting."

The bleak look in his eyes was almost more than she could bear. When he spoke, his voice was so low she had to strain to catch it. "We've been all through it so many times, Amanda. This is my life now." His eyes met hers. "Make me a promise."

Amanda knew this was a lousy time to be making promises, but she could not deny him. She loved the man and he was hurting. She was the one who had been attacked, but he was the one who was suffering far beyond her ability to understand it. "Anything," she agreed.

"I want you to take a class in self-defense and I want you to go with me to the gun range. I want to see how well you shoot and then I'm going to get you a gun. And I'm moving in whether you like it or not."

She decided to ignore the part about moving in. "I've taken self-defense classes," she reminded him, fighting her own panicky feelings to calm Donelli.

"Then you'll take another one. Promise me, Amanda."

"We'll talk about it later."

"Now. Promise. I have to know you can protect yourself."

There was no point in reminding him that all of his police training had not prevented the nearly fatal attacks on his life. Still, she felt the tension in his taut shoulders, saw the tight clenching of his jaw. She touched his cheek and met his gaze evenly. "I'll take the classes."

He sighed. Then, his hands gentle on her cheeks, he kissed her. When he spoke again his voice was under control, his expression neutral. "Amanda, try to remember what happened here tonight. It could be important. Detective Harrison's going to want to know when he gets here."

"You called him?"

"Of course, I called him. This was damned near a repeat of what happened to Carrie Owens."

Reluctantly, she struggled to match his cool demeanor. Whether he ever admitted it or not, this was Donelli the cop. He tempered his passionate professionalism with quiet compassion and maybe that was the problem. The compassion took too much out of him.

As she struggled to bring the last of the memories into

focus, the fog lifted. "Someone tried to smother me, the same way they did Carrie."

"I figured that much out. Did you see anyone when you came into the locker room? Hear anything?"

"Nothing," she said confidently, a little surprised at her own certainty. Whoever had attacked had been quick and clever. He—or she—had made only one mistake that she could see: he'd left before making absolutely certain that Amanda was dead. "There were a couple of women talking when I first came in, but they left."

"Are you sure both of them left?"

"I didn't see them, but it sounded like they were both going through the door when they said good night."

"Anything else?"

"There was a shower running."

"Did it shut off or did you hear the door open after they left?"

"I heard the door open," she said slowly. "The shower was still on. It must have been Frank. He must have figured out that I was onto the drug operation. He must have connected me to Jenny Lee, just like you warned me he would."

Donelli was shaking his head. "It wasn't Marquez. He was in the snack bar the whole time. When Larry caught a glimpse of you in the gym, he decided that he and Jenny Lee should stick around until you came out. They kept an eye on Marquez while they were waiting. The guy stayed right behind that counter. He was still there when I turned up a couple of minutes later. When I looked in the gym and didn't see you, I sent Jenny Lee into the locker room. She found you right outside the door to the steam room."

A knot formed in her stomach. "The steam room?" she repeated shakily.

"Yes." Donelli looked puzzled. "Why?"

"I was attacked right in front of my locker. Whoever it was must have been dragging me over here. When he heard Jenny Lee coming, he ran."

"Or hid in the sauna."

"Did you look?"

"No, forget it. He wouldn't have hid in there. There were half a dozen women in there when I got here. They came out when Jenny Lee screamed for me. Even if Frank had been able to slip out of sight for a few minutes, he wouldn't have risked coming into the women's locker room after you."

"No one noticed a man on the night Carrie was killed either," Amanda said slowly.

She and Donelli exchanged glances as a new piece of the puzzle fell into place.

"Alana," they said, practically in the same breath.

CHAPTER

Ten

Amanda looked around for Jenny Lee. She knew the would-be reporter wouldn't have vanished in the midst of all the excitement. She finally spotted her hovering on the fringes of the crowd, Larry by her side. She beckoned her over, reassured her several times that she was shaken but not seriously injured, then said, "See if you can get Frank and Alana's home address without Jackson figuring out what you're up to."

Jenny Lee seemed torn between delight at being granted this great responsibility and curiosity. The latter won. "Why?"

"Just do it, Jenny Lee," Donelli ordered impatiently, then grinned ruefully. "Sorry."

Jenny Lee smiled and gave his shoulder one of her maternal pats. "That's okay. You sound just like Oscar, all bark and no bite. He does that when he's worried about Amanda, too."

When she had gone, he said bemusedly, "Did she just insult me?"

Amanda chuckled. "No. She adores Oscar. She thinks he's the cutest little thing," she said, affecting Jenny Lee's southern accent.

"I assume she doesn't say that to his face."

"Are you kidding? He'd fire her on the spot."

Larry arrived just then, looking worried. He and Donelli assisted her onto one of the benches that stretched between the rows of lockers. Then he went to clear out the crowd of onlookers, who were still lingering in the doorway.

When he returned, his eyes were troubled. He picked up her hand and patted it awkwardly. "I'm sorry, Amanda. I guess I'm not so hot at this detective stuff. I should have guessed you were in trouble, when you didn't follow me out right away. Are you sure you're all right?"

"I'm fine. And it's not your fault. Besides, if you hadn't spotted me in here in the first place, Donelli might never have come looking for me. What happened with Frank? Did you find out anything about the drugs?"

"Oh, I'd have come looking," Donelli interrupted. "And if you hadn't already been passed out on the floor, I might have wrung your neck myself."

Amanda decided that Jenny Lee's return was particularly timely. Maybe she'd tell her about the drugs.

Instead, Jenny Lee blurted breathlessly, "You all will never guess who I just saw." Her hazel eyes were wide and sparkling with excitement. "Kelvin Washington."

Donelli and Larry looked unimpressed. Amanda just looked blank.

"Oh, Amanda, you know, that absolutely gorgeous hunk who plays football for the Georgia Bulldogs, the one they say is a shoo-in for the Heisman Trophy. I swear he is every bit as handsome as they say. Why he's got shoulders so broad, they practically fill the doorway."

Larry's expression was turning more sour by the second. Donelli merely looked amused.

"Jenny Lee, the address," Amanda reminded her. "Did you get it?"

Jenny Lee looked indignant. "Why, of course, I got it. That's what you sent me for, isn't it? Jackson was in his office and that sweet instructor who works the desk at night gave it right to me. He didn't even ask why I wanted it." She handed Amanda a slip of paper.

"And just where did you see this dumb jock?" Larry inquired.

"He was coming out of Jackson's office. You don't suppose he was signing up for a membership, do you?" She sounded ready to swoon. Then Amanda noted the calculated gleam in Jenny Lee's eyes and realized the performance was being given entirely for Larry's benefit. Judging from his scowl, the act was very effective.

"Why don't you two go on out to my place and wait for us," she suggested.

"Where are you going?" Jenny Lee wanted to know at once.

"We want to stop by Alana's." She glanced at Donelli. "And if we don't hurry, Detective Harrison will be rolling in here. He'll probably take a dim view of our going anywhere."

"Maybe we should stay, Amanda. The stakes have gone up. I'd like a little police protection for you," Donelli said.

"If things go all official now, we'll never get the answers. We'll talk to Harrison later. I promise. We need to see Alana now."

"Larry and I can come along," Jenny Lee volunteered.

"No. If all four of us descend on her at once, it'll scare her out of her wits. She'll never admit to anything. Besides, you'll be more help if you just stay here, tell the detective that the call was a false alarm and then go to my place."

Jenny Lee looked glum until Larry dropped an arm across her shoulders. "We'll do it, Amanda. Won't we, Jenny Lee?"

She beamed up at him. "Why, of course, we will."

As Amanda and Donelli hurried from the gym, he said, "Why do I have the feeling that Larry's about to spend the rest of his life in that same bewildered state of mind I'm usually in when you're around?"

Amanda grinned at him. "I know. Isn't it wonderful?"

"That's a matter of opinion," he grumbled as he slammed the door of his beloved Chevy harder than usual.

Frank and Alana's house was in the kind of subdivision that exists in every city—block after block of houses designed exactly alike except for the addition of an ornamental wall here or an iron railing there. The bright pink and blue and yellow used to paint the stucco did give them a sort of garish individuality. Bikes and toys were scattered on most of the tiny patches of lawn.

They found Alana in a salmon-colored house with a religious statue in the front yard and pots of bright red geraniums on the minuscule stoop. She didn't seem pleased to see them—or at least Amanda. For Donelli, there was a faint suggestion of a smile.

"What do you want?" She addressed the question to him.

"Just to talk," Donelli said.

"Why?"

"We were wondering where you were earlier this evening," Donelli said.

"Why would you want to know that?" she asked suspiciously.

"It's important, Alana, or we wouldn't be asking."

She sighed. "I was here all night with my grandmother. We are making a new dress." She opened the door wider. "Look. You see for yourself."

Indeed, a heavyset older woman, her black and gray hair pulled back severely from a still-handsome face, was sitting in front of an impressive sewing machine. Floral material was draped across her lap. Other pieces of the pattern were scattered on the floor. As an alibi, it was merely circumstantial, no more proof of innocence than Amanda's suppositions were proof of guilt.

"Can we come in?" she asked.

With great reluctance, Alana finally agreed. She sent her grandmother off to the kitchen with a rapid spate of Spanish that Amanda thought had something to do with coffee. She guessed the woman was either supposed to drink it or serve it.

"What do you really want?" Alana demanded when her grandmother had gone.

Amanda decided to be direct. "Someone attacked me at the club tonight, the same way they killed Carrie Owens."

Alana looked genuinely shocked. "Who would do such a thing? It was Roberto, like before?"

"Alana, we have no proof it was Roberto, then or now. No one noticed a man in the locker room either night."

"Which leads us to wonder if it might not have been a woman," Donelli said.

Alana looked even more suspicious. "You asked before where I was tonight. You think I am the one, don't you? *Madre de Dios* . . ." She went off in a tirade of Spanish that Amanda was sure would have blistered their ears, if they'd understood it. Sparks danced in Alana's dark eyes.

"Why would I do it?" she demanded. "You tell me that, you are so smart? Why?"

"There were rumors about Carrie and your husband," Amanda said bluntly.

She waved a hand dismissively. "Talk, all talk. I know about these rumors."

"And they didn't upset you?"

"*Sí*. At first I wanted to see her dead. And why not?" she said defensively. "I hear the talk about Carrie and my Frank. Everyone says they are lovers. In my heart I know better. But I do not like the humiliation. Everyone is so sure that my Frank is cheating on me. It makes me a little crazy."

"Then you were jealous," Amanda said.

She waved her hand in the air in another gesture of dismissal. "*Por nada*. For nothing. Frank explained to me what he was doing."

"And what was that?"

"He said he was afraid for her. He thought she was interfering in things that were none of her concern. He was talking to her, trying to make her see that she was being foolish."

"What things?"

"*No sé*. I don't know. He wouldn't tell me. He said if he told me, then I would be in as much danger as Carrie."

"And you believed him?"

"Why wouldn't I? She is dead now, isn't she?"

Admittedly, it was a convincing argument, but Amanda knew that Frank could have been twisting the truth to keep Alana from going after both him and Carrie. His wife had a volatile temper that equaled his own. Still, the explanation did seem to fit with what the waitress at the coffee shop had told her. Perhaps Frank had simply been trying to warn Carrie about something. The image of Frank as a nice guy was hard to believe, but she saw no point in trying to get Alana to attack her husband's personality. She was obviously very loyal.

"Thanks, Alana," she said finally.

"*De nada*." She spoke with little sincerity, but at the door, some of the anger faded from her eyes. She cautiously reached out and touched Amanda's arm. "Be careful, *señorita*. I am sorry for what happened to you."

Minutes later, Donelli headed for I-285. On the drive around the perimeter highway, they were silent. Finally he asked, "Did you believe her?"

Amanda sighed. "Surprisingly enough, yes. Oh, I think she's more than capable of killing someone in a jealous rage, but I also think she believed Frank when he made excuses for getting close to Carrie. What do you think?"

"I agree with you."

"So, we're right back where we started."

"Not entirely. Who else had access to that locker room the night Carrie was killed and again tonight?"

"It's a locker room, Donelli. Not Fort Knox. Everyone who belongs had access."

"Not everyone. It was the women's locker room, remember."

Despite Donelli's apparent satisfaction with whatever point he was trying to make, Amanda could not see it. "We don't even have another female suspect," she said glumly. "We're even worse off than ever."

"Who said anything about another woman? There are two men whose presence in there wouldn't be questioned."

Understanding dawned. "Jackson and Robert," she said, her excitement suddenly mounting.

"Exactly."

"And I know Jackson was at the club tonight right before I was attacked because he made a point of reminding me that I'd stayed on the exercise bike too long."

"He was also there afterward, if Jenny Lee was right

about Kelvin Washington being in his office. If he'd tried to kill you, I doubt if he would have stuck around. What about Robert?"

"He wasn't there tonight. At least, I didn't see him. The night Carrie was killed, he came in when the police called him. They couldn't find Jackson."

"Maybe we should pay a little visit to the two of them."

"Starting with?"

"Robert. He had a lot to say about his partner the last time we met with him. Maybe he'll be even more expansive tonight."

Donelli turned his aging Chevy back toward Atlanta. Amanda had once sworn never to ride in the dented heap again, especially with Donelli behind the wheel. His idea of speed was only one or two miles per hour faster than parking. It drove her crazy.

Tonight was no different. Donelli was creeping along. To top it off, he switched on a country music station. The mournful words and twanging guitars strummed across her nerves like chalk squeaking on a blackboard. If he was trying to get even with her, he couldn't have chosen a more effective way.

"Can't you drive a little faster?" she snapped impatiently.

"Why? We're not going to a fire. I doubt if Robert suspects we're coming to visit. The last time we talked to him he seemed fairly confident that he'd steered us off on the wrong track. Besides, if he had anything to do with attacking you tonight, he left before he realized you survived."

Amanda glared at him, but she bit back another comment about Donelli's driving. That's why she was so surprised when she saw the police car in the side mirror. Its lights were flashing. It was crawling at the same pace they were.

"I think you'd better check the rearview mirror," she said.

"What the hell?" Donelli muttered.

"Maybe he wants to arrest you for slowing down traffic," Amanda suggested sweetly.

"Cute, Amanda." He pulled the car to the side of the road, then waited for the policeman to approach. Instead the officer used a bullhorn to request that they leave the vehicle.

"Put your hands out where I can see them," he ordered.

Suddenly Amanda did not see the humor in the situation either. She shot a questioning glance at Donelli. He motioned for her to get out, but she could tell from the set of his mouth and the glint in his eyes that he was furious. She began to see charges of false arrest being slapped on the hapless officer who was finally swaggering toward them.

"What's the problem, Officer?" Donelli asked with barely concealed hostility.

"Just got a report a little while ago says this car is transporting drugs."

"What!" The word exploded from her and Donelli simultaneously.

"I'd like to see some ID, please."

Donelli extracted his wallet, which fortunately still contained his police identification from Brooklyn. That gave the policeman a moment's pause. Amanda expected a quick apology. Instead, the man's florid face took on a nasty expression.

"Nothing I hate worse than a dirty cop," he said.

Donelli tensed. Tiny white lines appeared at the corners of his mouth. His hands clenched.

"You're looking at a slander suit," he said with astonishing calm. "Along with false arrest and harassment."

"Ain't nothing false about it, if I find them drugs in your car. Now why don't we go take a look? You two get over here where I can keep an eye on you."

The policeman watched them closely as he went over the car from the front bumper to the taillights. When he unscrewed the cover on the left taillight, Amanda saw his mood improve visibly. Hers sank.

"Well, well, well, what have we here? Looks like cocaine to me. Wouldn't you say so, *Detective* Donelli?"

Amanda had remained silent as long as she could. She was not going to let this cocky imbecile charge them with possession of drugs.

"Those drugs were planted there," she said. "Whoever placed that call to the police wanted to see us arrested because we were getting too close to the truth about a drug operation here in town. Can't you see that? I mean, a taillight is a dumb place to try to hide drugs. Almost any imbecile—"

"Amanda!" Donelli's tone was unexpectedly sharp.

She bit back the insult before the policeman found some

way to use that against them too. He would probably turn it into a resisting arrest charge.

"Why don't you two folks just climb on in my car and we'll take a little ride down to the station."

It was a rhetorical question, since he was already shoving them into the backseat of the cruiser. The locks clicked into place. They sounded only slightly less ominous than the clanging of a jail-cell door. Amanda recalled an interview she once did in a state penitentiary. Only after she'd left had she realized that she hadn't drawn an easy breath the entire time she'd been inside. Her chest felt the same constriction now.

She reached across and put her hand in Donelli's. He squeezed it, making her feel safer, although it did not wake her from the nightmare, which she had a feeling was only just beginning.

There was something almost comforting, though, about the familiarity of the police station. The flourescent lighting cast a stark blue tint over everything. It was not an effect designed to do wonders for the complexion, which was probably why mug shots could make a clean-cut Wall Street broker look like a criminal, which, of course, he sometimes was. The place was also noisy, a blend of ringing phones, shuffling papers, muted conversations, and occasional shrill bursts of outrage or drug-induced psychosis. It was littered with discarded coffee cups, crumpled cigarette packs, and mangled soft drink cans. It was not unlike a newsroom.

The minute they were "introduced" to the desk sergeant, Amanda insisted on calling Detective Jim Harrison for the second time that night. He probably would not be thrilled that she skipped out on him earlier at Weights and Measures, but she had no doubt that he would come. She also wanted to call a lawyer and Oscar. Without delay.

The sergeant, David Kennedy according to the name-plate on the desk, blinked at her requests. Donelli actually grinned at his bemused expression. In fact, Amanda decided, Donelli seemed to be enjoying this slightly more than he should be for a man who had just been arrested for possession of cocaine.

"You only get one call, Amanda," he reminded her.

"So do you. I'll call Oscar. You call the lawyer." She smiled beguilingly at Sergeant Kennedy, whose ears turned red. "You can call Detective Harrison."

The sergeant, who was considerably more accommodating than the arresting officer, pointed to a pay phone. He even dug in his pocket for a quarter. "Help yourself, ma'am."

She wasn't wild about his use of *ma'am* to address her. She blamed the flourescent lighting.

A half hour later all three men had responded to Amanda's alarm. Oscar came in with his shirttail hanging loose, his tie askew, and his socks mismatched. She shook her head. He looked as though he had dressed in a hurry, selecting his clothes from the laundry hamper. But, then again, she'd seen him look the same way by lunchtime. The lawyer, one of Donelli's friends from Gwinnett County, appeared sleepy. Only Detective Harrison strolled in as if there was nothing the least bit unusual about being dragged down to a precinct house at eleven at night by an ex-cop and a reporter, who were for the moment on the wrong side of the law.

"What the hell's going on here?" Oscar said. He moved protectively to Amanda's side, for which she decided she owed him at the very least a bottle of twelve-year-old Chivas Regal and forty-eight hours of no grumbling.

Everyone tried to answer the question at once, creating an ear-shattering cacophony. Detective Harrison brought about order by raising one hand and staring the rest of them down. It was a very successful technique. He was probably a wonderful father. In fact, he could probably take on an entire boarding school of unruly teens.

"Why don't I take Mr. Donelli and Ms. Roberts into one of the conference rooms and chat with them?" he suggested. "Maybe we can get to the bottom of this."

Sergeant Kennedy looked disappointed, but nodded agreeably enough.

The attorney wanted to come, too. Detective Harrison shrugged indifferently. He looked at Donelli. "It's up to you."

"I think he'd better come."

That left Oscar. Amanda saw the expression in his eyes. He was chomping at the bit to get a piece of this action. "I want Oscar in there."

Detective Harrison sighed. "Well, hail, hail," he said wearily. "It looks like the gang's all here. Let's go."

It took a few minutes to restore order and establish that only one person was going to be permitted to talk at a time. To Amanda's frustration, it appeared that Donelli was to be given center stage. He was just going to report the facts, while she had several instincts she wanted to share.

"Tell me exactly what happened tonight," the detective suggested.

In a flat, unemotional voice Donelli began with Amanda's suspicion that drugs were being sold through the snack bar at Weights and Measures. When he explained about the decision to send Larry to test the theory, the attorney looked stunned.

"What the hell were the two of you thinking about?" he said, then clamped his mouth shut when Detective Harrison scowled.

"What the hell *were* the two of you thinking about?" the detective echoed. "Does this have anything to do with that call I responded to earlier tonight, the one in which the victim had vanished?" He stared pointedly at Amanda.

Amanda opened her mouth to explain and to take the blame, but Donelli shot her a warning glance. "We thought we could get some evidence to turn over to you," he said.

Harrison feigned shock. "You were doing that for us? How helpful! I do so wish more citizens would get involved."

Amanda thought the sarcasm was a little overdone.

"So you sent this kid down there to check things out. Then what happened?"

"Amanda went down to watch," Donelli reported in a resigned tone. "Someone attacked her in the locker room and tried to smother her the same way they had Carrie Owens."

Detective Harrison obviously wasn't surprised by this

bit of news. Neither was Oscar. Apparently Larry had reached him earlier and explained the outcome of their little foray into the snack bar. The attorney, however, looked dazed. She had a hunch his practice consisted mostly of fighting traffic tickets and drawing up wills.

"I suppose you think you know who was responsible," the detective said.

"We thought it might be Alana Marquez, but she denied it. As near as we could tell that left only two possibilities. We were on our way to check one of them out, when we were stopped. Someone had tipped the cops about the cocaine in the car. It was obviously a set up."

"Unless, of course, you decided to keep the cocaine you had your friend buy and put it in the taillight yourself for safekeeping."

Amanda jumped up. Her voice shook with indignation. "We did not keep the damn cocaine."

"Then where is it?"

That drew her up short. "I assume Larry still has it. Maybe he's already turned it in. I don't know," she admitted with great reluctance.

"Then I'd suggest you sit back down," Detective Harrison said.

Grinding her teeth, she sat.

"We think the cocaine at Weights and Measures is being sold in tiny packets done up to look like those sugar packets you see in restaurants," Donelli said.

"Where's this Larry now?"

"At my place," Amanda volunteered.

Detective Harrison picked up a phone and repeated that

information to the desk sergeant. "Get someone over there to check it out."

In the meantime, they all sat and stared at each other. It was nearly an hour before the phone rang. The detective picked it up.

"Harrison here. Yeah. Okay. Okay. Thanks. No problem. Okay."

Amanda squirmed. It was not exactly an illuminating conversation on this end. Detective Harrison's expression never changed. He looked tired, and impatient, and glum.

"Well?" Donelli said, when he'd hung up.

"We found the packets. Your friends had them, just like you said."

"And?"

"They were filled with sugar."

Oh, hell.

CHAPTER Eleven

For the first time since Amanda had known him, Oscar appeared to have been rendered speechless. Vanishing cocaine was apparently more than even he could try to explain away. Dollar signs seemed to glitter in the attorney's suddenly wide awake eyes as he apparently contemplated a lengthy case. Amanda felt as though the floor had dropped out from under her and she was dangling over a pit of vipers. She was furious with herself for not demanding more answers from Larry and Jenny Lee earlier. Only Donelli was actually smiling.

Smiling? She stared at him more closely on the off chance that he was in shock. He appeared, though, to be genuinely amused by this latest turn of events. His sense of humor eluded her completely at times.

"You didn't really expect to find cocaine in those packets, did you?" he inquired with such nonchalance that Amanda wondered if he'd managed to sneak a beer or two sometime during the troubled course of the evening.

"Donelli!" she hissed urgently. He ignored her. As usual.

"If someone knew enough to set me up, they also knew enough to get rid of the evidence at the health club. It'll probably be the cleanest place in town until this whole thing blows over."

Amanda brightened. "Of course." She turned to Oscar. "That makes sense, doesn't it?"

"Absolutely," Oscar said gruffly. His voice lacked confidence and he still looked as though his head were reeling. He peered at the detective for confirmation. "What do you think?"

All eyes were on Detective Harrison, who for once did not seem overly fond of the spotlight. He fidgeted and drew little circles on a scratch pad, then finally looked up and met Oscar's hopeful gaze.

"Actually finding the cocaine in the sugar packets was a long shot," he admitted, then glanced at Donelli and Amanda in turn. "But I thought you two could use a little luck about now. Looks as though the charges will have to stick for the moment. We'll get a judge to set bail in the morning."

"Bail?" Amanda repeated with an uncharacteristic squeak in her voice. Then the full impact of what was happening sank in. "You're actually arresting us?"

"You've already been arrested. We're booking you."

"On what charge? Never mind. I know the answer to that. What I don't know is how the hell you can think it'll hold up in court." She gestured toward Donelli. "This man's a policeman."

"*Was* a policeman, Amanda," Donelli reminded her with an extraordinarily crummy sense of timing.

She scowled back at him. "This is no time to be bringing up that stupid retirement." She turned back to Detective Harrison, who seemed fascinated by the exchange. "I'm a reporter. I'm working this story. The only thing you have on me is circumstantial at best. It wasn't even my car."

"Amanda, are you jumping from a sinking ship?" Donelli inquired lightly. She flushed at the charge until she saw that he was chuckling. He took her hand and patted it. She hated it when he patronized her. She tried snatching her hand back, but he held on tight.

"It's okay," he soothed. "We'll spend one night in jail. Tomorrow we'll get out of here and track down the person responsible."

Detective Harrison started shaking his head before Donelli could even complete the sentence. "Uh-uh. You two are going to keep your noses out of this. If you'd done that in the first place, you wouldn't be in this mess."

"If we'd done that in the first place, you wouldn't know about the drug operation," Amanda snapped.

"What drug operation?" the detective replied smugly. "Looks to me like it's gone underground . . . if it even existed in the first place."

"Oh, it existed," Amanda retorted. "You can bet we're going to prove that."

Detective Harrison smiled at her. There was frost around the edges of that smile. "If you don't promise to back off, I can see to it that your bail is so high, it'd take a Colombian drug lord to get you out of here," he said politely.

Amanda shut up, but she was fuming. She also was making no promises she wouldn't keep.

Oscar whispered to the attorney. The attorney cleared his throat. "Um, don't you think maybe we could take care of this matter tonight? I mean these two people aren't exactly criminals, are they? They have jobs."

At least one of us does, Amanda thought.

Oscar grew impatient with the attorney's lackluster style. "Come on, Harrison, you'll never get those charges to stick and you know it. Save the taxpayers the cost of their breakfast and let them go. I'll vouch for them."

The detective looked torn. He obviously relished the idea of seeing Amanda and Donelli behind bars, if only for a night. He seemed to have the crazy notion that it would teach them a much-needed lesson. At the same time, he also knew that Oscar had a point. Amanda held her breath while he decided their fate—their immediate fate, she corrected. Hopefully, their long-term fate was out of his hands.

"Okay," he said at last. "Clear out of here, but if I so much as hear a whisper about the two of you poking your noses in where they don't belong, I'll make tonight's interrogation seem like party chitchat. Am I making myself clear?"

"Absolutely," said the lawyer.

"No problem," promised Oscar.

Amanda and Donelli wisely kept their mouths shut.

Outside police headquarters, the lawyer wandered off, still yawning. Oscar glared at the two of them, taking up where Detective Harrison had left off.

"I'll see you in my office at nine," he said. The order was directed at Amanda. She winced at his tone. She'd never heard him quite so furious.

"I'll be there," she said meekly.

"As for you," he said to Donelli, "I wouldn't blame you for going after whoever set you up, but leave her out of it."

Donelli grinned. "I think you're telling that to the wrong person."

"Oh, don't you worry about that," Oscar growled. "I'll say all that and more when I see her in the morning."

"Would you two kindly stop talking as if I've already been sent off to bed without my supper? I'm here. I can speak for myself."

"I'd suggest you save it for morning," Donelli said quietly. His gaze shifted pointedly to Oscar.

She took another look at Oscar and saw the wisdom of heeding Donelli's advice. "Right. Nine o'clock."

Without uttering another word, Oscar dropped them at Weights and Measures so they could pick up Amanda's car. With Donelli behind the wheel, it took them over an hour to get home, even though there was little traffic on the highway. Amanda was tense and exhausted by the time he turned into her driveway. When she saw Larry's car parked outside, she groaned.

"I forgot all about Larry and Jenny Lee. I'm not sure I can deal with them at this hour."

"As soon as we find out what happened in that snack bar fiasco tonight, we'll send them home."

Recalling that disaster snapped Amanda awake again.

Inside, they found Jenny Lee curled up on the sofa sound asleep. Larry was watching over her like a guardian angel. He touched a finger to his lips and motioned toward the kitchen, but before they could sit down at the round oak table, Jenny Lee appeared in the doorway, yawning and rubbing her eyes like a tired child.

"Don't even think about leaving me out of this," she said between yawns.

Amanda glanced at the clock and sighed. It was already after three o'clock. With two versions of the story to hear instead of one, it was going to be a long session. "I'll make coffee. It doesn't look as though any of us are likely to sleep tonight."

"I might as well make sandwiches too," Jenny Lee offered.

When everyone was settled at the table with food and coffee strong enough to jar the most sluggish brain into action, Donelli said, "Okay, what happened in that snack bar tonight? Did Marquez seem at all suspicious?"

"Not one bit," Larry said. "In fact, the whole thing was a piece of cake. I met this kid outside. We talked a little and he took me in. Then Jenny Lee came along and we all ordered."

"A straight order? Or was there some sort of code involved?"

"That's the funny part. The kid seemed to know exactly what I meant when I hinted around about getting something really special inside. I said I'd heard this was the place to come. He said he'd take care of it. He ordered for all three of us. We left and took our part of the order. Jenny Lee went and put it into the car, while I watched for Amanda. You know what happened after that. It wasn't until we got back here that I even looked in the bag. I felt like a jerk.

There wasn't anything the least bit suspicious in the bag. When the cops showed up asking about the sugar packets, it dawned on me that that could be the way they were selling the drugs. But when we opened the packets, nothing. Just ordinary sugar."

"But you don't think Frank was on to you," Amanda insisted.

"If he was, he sure as hell can act."

Jenny Lee confirmed it. "You know how much I'm in there, Amanda. Frank didn't act one bit different than he has any other night. He was cool, polite, and helpful. If he was expecting a sting, he definitely didn't show it."

"But why would he put the sugar in the bag in the first place? I saw what you ordered to drink. Just apple juice and sparkling water."

Jenny Lee closed her eyes and groaned. "Is that what gave you the idea there was cocaine in those packets? That was my fault. I told him I was going to make tea. He offered to throw in some sugar."

"So much for that theory," Amanda said, shaking her head at the absurd way she had assumed too much, too quickly. "Now I feel like an idiot."

"But I could have sworn that kid actually understood what I was talking about," Larry countered. "There has to be something going on. We just screwed it up tonight."

"Maybe it was the kid, then. Maybe he was suspicious," Donelli suggested. "Maybe he didn't want to be responsible for blowing the place's cover."

"Or maybe we've gotten off on the wrong track entirely. Maybe there are no drugs," Amanda said reluctantly. At

Donelli's stunned look, she said, "I know. I'm the one who was convinced, but maybe I jumped to the wrong conclusion. Let's just go back to what we do know."

"Which is?" Jenny Lee said.

Amanda enumerated. "One, Carrie Owens was murdered. Two, she may have known something about the club that got her killed. And three, there's a duplicate set of books, one of which has been tampered with to suggest that the income is greater than it really is. Everything else is unsubstantiated . . . the drugs, Carrie's affair with Frank, even the fights between Jackson and Robert."

Larry looked disgusted. "That's it? I hate to say this, Amanda, but you don't know a thing to connect anyone to Carrie Owens's murder."

"You don't have to rub it in."

Donelli, who'd remained silent for a long time, said, "That's not entirely true. We know a lot. We're just not sure how it fits together."

"So what do we do now?" Larry asked.

"In the same tedious way cops have to put every case together. I'll keep on assembling little pieces of information, no matter how inconsequential they may seem. Sooner or later, they'll add up."

Amanda stared at him. "Does that mean you're really going to get involved now and help us?"

Donelli returned the look evenly. "I don't think I have any choice. I'm already involved. You were nearly killed tonight. That cocaine was planted in my car, so someone obviously knew what we suspected. That means we're getting close. Tomorrow I'm going to have a talk with

Jackson and Robert. It's about time I started putting my fifteen years with the Brooklyn police to good use."

"What about the rest of us?" Jenny Lee said. "What do you want us to do?"

"Stay out of it." He was adamant.

"But—" Amanda began.

"I mean it. I can't protect all of you, if you're going to go off snooping on your own. Leave the detective work to me and get back to your own professions."

"He's right," Larry said, directing the remark to Jenny Lee, who was looking especially disappointed. "Let's get out of here. I have an assignment for the *Gazette* first thing this morning, and I'd like to get home and change before I go. You coming, Jenny Lee?"

After a hopeful look at Donelli, who said nothing, then at Amanda, who remained equally silent, she shrugged. "I guess I might as well."

When they'd gone, Amanda moved to Donelli's lap. She put her arms around his neck and kissed his cheek. He turned his head and captured the second kiss with his lips. Fire leapt through her veins at once. The breath-stealing kiss was filled with hunger and urgency fueled by days of denial. When Donelli put his mind to it, he could make her toes curl. Her heart was thumping hard enough to provide the beat for a rock tune. She felt vibrantly alive. After her terror in the locker room, she needed very much to experience such life-affirming sensations. But just as her body began to respond to Donelli's provocative kisses, he sighed and placed one last chaste kiss on her forehead, then rested his forehead against her cheek.

"What was that for?" she asked in a ragged whisper.

One corner of his mouth tilted up. "You started it, Amanda."

She smiled and feathered more kisses along his jaw. "So I did. Perhaps I should finish it." She ran her tongue lightly across his bottom lip. She could feel his muscles tighten, the swift surge of his arousal against her hip.

"Don't do that unless you mean it," he warned lightly.

"Oh, I mean it."

"I'm serious. You're the one who put distance between us because we had problems. Do you think they're resolved?"

She sighed. "No, but I am glad we're really going to be working together for a change, instead of being at odds."

He scowled. "That's not reason enough for us to start sleeping together again."

He was right, damn it. Still she asked, "Don't you want me?" She knew the answer to that, but she needed to hear him say it. If he wouldn't make love to her tonight, she needed desperately to know that he wanted to as badly as she wanted him to.

"Don't ever doubt that," he said, his fingers gentle against her cheek. His eyes blazed with desire. "I want you so much my entire body aches right now."

She considered that sufficient invitation for one more try for the intimacy they both craved, but he lifted her up and sat her back on her own chair. He loomed over her. It was his favorite posture for lecturing and for attempting to intimidate a prospective partner. Apparently he planned to change the subject.

"We are not going to be working together, Amanda," he said slowly, giving each word a subtle emphasis. "Didn't you hear anything I said a minute ago when Jenny Lee and Larry were here?"

"But I thought you just said that for their benefit. Looking into this is my profession, too."

"I don't recall mentioning any exclusions. This is a criminal investigation."

"It has always been a criminal investigation," she reminded him. "That's why it's going to make such a damned good story."

"If you want to do a story when things are all wrapped up, fine. I'll give you any information you want."

"Who made you press officer for the Atlanta PD? As you have repeatedly reminded me, you are no longer a police officer. If you ask me, that makes my position slightly more legitimate than yours. I am a working member of the media."

"There are lots of other stories, Amanda. Don't you still have that article on the historic homes to do?"

"Oscar gives me my assignments, Donelli. Until he says otherwise, I am working on this one," she said confidently.

"I saw the look in Oscar's eyes tonight when we left the police station. If I were you, I wouldn't wager your next paycheck on covering this story," Donelli advised before stalking off. "I'm going to get a couple of hours of sleep. The way things are going, I'll need it."

She stared after him and fumed. She absolutely hated men who wouldn't stick around to let her have the last word. It didn't help that he was apparently going to sleep in her bed after telling her not five minutes ago that they shouldn't be sleeping together. Where the hell did he expect her to sleep? The sofa? Fat chance.

Still, crawling into bed beside him required extraordinary self-control. One part of her wanted to slap him awake and tell him exactly what she thought of his high-handedness. The other part wanted to finish up the steamy tenderness they had begun in the kitchen. She decided, instead, to try pretending that he wasn't even there, which was virtually impossible since the mattress dipped significantly under his weight. She had to concentrate very hard to remain on her own side of the bed. She glared at his back. It looked solid and warm and inviting.

"Oh, to hell with it," she muttered, curving herself against him. With a tiny sigh of contentment, she fell asleep.

It seemed as though she had barely closed her eyes, when she awoke with a start, her heart hammering. There wasn't a sound in the room. The digital clock by the bed cast an eerie green glow. It was 4:57. She had been in bed less than twenty minutes. She yawned and rolled over, instinctively seeking the comfort of Donelli's arms.

He was gone.

That's what had awakened her. She was alone in the bed again. She got up, grabbed an oversized T-shirt from the back of a chair and tugged it over her head. "Joe? Where are you?"

She padded through the living room and saw that the front door was open. She crossed over quietly and peered into the inky darkness. She heard the creak of the rocker before she saw him. Shoulders hunched, he was staring pensively ahead. The rhythm of the rocker was slow and even, apparently keeping time with his troubled thoughts.

"You okay?" she asked quietly.

"Fine."

"Couldn't you sleep?"

"Something woke me up."

Something in his voice, the slightest catch, scared her. She went outside. The air was fragrant with honeysuckle, the porch damp with dew. She drew in a deep breath.

"Go back to bed," he urged.

Instead she walked over and knelt by the rocker, resting her head on his knees. "Tell me what woke you."

His hand idly caressed her hair. He was silent for so long, though, she thought he wasn't going to answer. Finally, he sighed heavily. "I had a dream."

The raw pain in his voice alerted her. "A nightmare?"

"Oh, yeah, it was a nightmare all right."

"Tell me about it."

"What's the point? It was only a dream."

"Was it?"

"What is that supposed to mean?"

"Exactly what I said. If it was only a dream, you wouldn't be this disturbed."

"Oh, really? When did you get your Ph.D. in psychology? Or did that come with the law degree and the journalism degree? Just one of those package deals they offer for the brightest and best."

Hurt by his cynical tone, she sat up, drew her knees to her chest and wrapped her arms around them. "God, I hate it when you get like this. My education is not the issue here. Something's upset you. I want to know what it is because I care, not because I get my kicks by making you bare your soul. Can't you see that?"

After a long, frightening silence, he reached out and drew her head back to his knee. He brushed a tendril of hair back from her face with incredible tenderness. The work-roughened pads of his fingers rasped across her skin bringing it alive. The slightest touch, she thought in wonder. That's all it took between them to stir the magic.

"I thought I was back out in the streets," he said finally. His flat tone warned her that he was about to replace wonder with harsh reality. Her stomach clenched in anticipation. "There was this kid. He was high on drugs. He had a knife and he went for me. Then he went for my partner."

Amanda felt a lump form in her throat. She knew the conclusion of the story. Donelli had ended up with a nearly fatal knife wound. His partner had not been as lucky. Vicky Markham had died. He had worked with her and cared about her and he hadn't been able to stop her from dying. Now that he had started, she wanted him to stop. "You don't have to finish. I know the rest."

The dam was broken, though, and the words poured out. Angry words filled with self-loathing. "Do you really? Do you know how I felt tonight when I found you lying on the floor in that locker room? Do you know what I would have done if I could have gotten my hands on the person who attacked you? When you're in danger the way you are now, I don't just want to protect you. It goes way beyond that. I feel rage. I want to get even. What kind of cop would that make me, Amanda? What kind of cop wants vengeance instead of justice?''

Tears threatened to spill down her cheeks, but she didn't want to show weakness now, when Donelli so obviously needed her strength for a change. She took his hand and held it tight. She kissed the scarred knuckles. "A very human cop, Joe."

"Don't you see, though, Amanda, I can't go back. I'd be a menace. I probably shouldn't even get involved in this investigation, especially since you're a target. It's like doctors not operating on a member of their own family. There's no cool objectivity."

"I think in your heart you know that isn't true. Your values are too deeply ingrained for you to take the law into your own hands. But maybe I've been wrong to push you so. Maybe you do need more time to get your perspective back, to heal after what happened to Vicky."

"Vicky was killed nearly three years ago. Isn't that long enough? Shouldn't I have forgotten by now? I can still see her falling. I can still feel what it was like lying there, knowing I couldn't get to her."

"And what happened to me tonight brought it all back," she said with regret. At last she was beginning to comprehend what she put him through with her stubborn recklessness. "Joe, I understand now why you hover over me, why you feel such a need to protect those you love. But you won't let it get out of hand, and I'll try to be more careful. I really will. Don't let the past rob you of something that's as important to you as your work."

He managed a sad smile. "But you said it yourself, Amanda, it's not just the past anymore."

At nine o'clock, groggy from lack of sleep and worried about Donelli's inner torment, Amanda eased warily into Oscar's office. He looked up from the page proofs he was reading and frowned.

"Sit. I'll be done in a minute."

Amanda sat. She brushed imaginary lint from her black linen skirt. She fiddled with the bow at the collar of her blouse. She crossed her legs, then uncrossed them. She got up and poured herself a cup of coffee from the pot Oscar kept on a hot plate. The movement attracted his attention for an instant, then he went back to editing.

Finally, when Amanda was considering stomping out of the office in a huff, he tucked his pencil behind his ear and leaned back in his chair.

"What is one of the first tenets of good journalism?" he asked in a professorial tone that was as incongruous coming from Oscar as it would have been from Donelli. In fact, it was something she might have expected from Mack, who was used to talking that way to his students. Still, Amanda saw no point in aggravating Oscar's already foul mood by telling him he was acting exactly like her stuffy ex-husband.

"Objectivity," she said, thinking of Donelli's cry in the night for the same thing.

"Objectivity," he repeated, obviously pleased that she

recalled the concept. "No preconceived notions. No emotional ties to the story. No conflict of interest. Right?"

"Yes."

"Can you honestly tell me that you can be objective about this Carrie Owens thing?" His voice rose to a roar that echoed off the walls.

"Of course, I can," she said indignantly.

He swallowed hard and made an attempt to calm down. That alone was enough to terrify her. An irate, blowing-off-steam Oscar was someone she understood, someone she could bargain with. Controlled fury suggested he was in command in a way she'd never before encountered.

"Oh, really?" he said. "You've been threatened and attacked, presumably by someone connected to the case, unless there's someone else you've been offending that I don't know about. Am I being accurate so far?"

She felt her face flush, but she bit her tongue.

"Now your boyfriend is hauled in for possession of cocaine, another incident which is quite likely tied to the case." He leaned forward. Now his face was red. "And you have the nerve to tell me you can be objective?"

"Yes," she repeated adamantly.

Her reply was drowned out by Oscar's shout. "No! It can't be done. I want you off this story as of this moment. I want you to get busy on that feature I assigned you. I want it on my desk by the end of the week. And if I so much as hear you've touched a barbell at Weights and Measures, I will suspend you without pay. Am I making myself clear?"

"Have you been talking to Donelli?"

"No. I have not been talking to Donelli. Now answer me. Have I made myself clear?"

Amanda felt as though the wind had been knocked out of her. She had never been yanked off a story during her entire career. It was especially humiliating because she was convinced Oscar's decision had nothing to do with her objectivity. He was selling out, giving in to the police, maybe even Donelli, all of whom wanted her as far away from this story as possible. Her own anger began to mount, but it hadn't quite reached the same feverish pitch as Oscar's. She waited for her blood to reach boiling. Just as it did, the phone rang.

Oscar grabbed it and snapped, "Yes."

Amanda tapped her foot impatiently. She couldn't wait to tell Oscar exactly what she thought of his cowardly ultimatum. She was not worrying about phrasing it politely either. If he fired her, too bad. She didn't want to work for a man who was less interested in the truth than he was in pleasing the authorities.

"Yeah, I know about it," Oscar growled, shooting a pointed glance in her direction. "I'm taking care of it."

Suddenly his complexion went from red to splotchy purple. "Listen, Crenshaw, I make the editorial decisions around here or I'm out the door. That's the agreement we had."

That got Amanda's full attention. Her temper cooled as she listened more intently.

"I know. I hear what you're saying, but I haven't heard one good reason to kill that story. In fact, you've aroused my curiosity. If someone's so afraid of *Inside Atlanta* that they're running to you, then we must be getting close to something very big.''

Amanda heard an explosion of indignation over the phone. Oscar was grinning now. ''Is that an order, Crenshaw?''

Amanda held her breath and waited. Oscar's grin widened. ''I didn't think so. I'll keep you posted.''

When he'd hung up, Amanda said, ''Well?''

He stared at the ceiling for a full five minutes before sighing heavily.

''Oscar?''

He looked worried. ''I hope I don't regret this.''

''Regret what?''

''Get out there and find out who killed Carrie Owens and why.''

Her pulse raced. Amanda knew she shouldn't look a gift horse in the mouth, but she had to know exactly what had brought on Oscar's sudden change of heart. ''You just told me to drop it. Why the sudden turnaround?''

''Because someone's running scared. You know that was Crenshaw, and I'm sure you gathered that he wanted me to insist that you back off the story.''

''So now you want me to pursue it? What happened to all that stuff about objectivity?''

He glowered at her. ''Hell, Amanda, I know you could be objective if the story involved your own mother. I had to say something. I don't like all this stuff that's been happening to you.''

''So you were trying to protect me?'' she said incredulously.

He looked embarrassed. ''Something like that.''

She shook her head in amazement. "I don't believe it. If you and Donelli had your way, I'd never drive to the grocery store for milk. Honestly, Oscar, I appreciate your concern, but I can handle myself."

"Tell that to the guy who almost killed you last night," he said gruffly.

"I dropped my guard. It won't happen again."

He waved a finger at her. "See that it doesn't. I'd hate for that cop of yours to blame me if that pretty little neck of yours gets caught in a noose."

"I'll take care of Donelli," she vowed, then wondered how the hell she was going to do that. In her attempt to reassure him early this morning, she'd virtually promised him that she would back off the investigation or at least limit her role in pursuing the story. He was going to be livid when he realized she was not only going on with the story, but that she was doing it with Oscar's blessing.

It was only after she was back at her desk going over her notes, a tart lime jelly bean in her mouth, that the full impact of that phone conversation in Oscar's office came to her. She almost choked on the jelly bean.

Only one person was likely to have sufficient clout to get Joel Crenshaw to intercede in the editorial decisions of the magazine—Trace Weston.

Perhaps it was time to pay another visit to the corporate tycoon. Or perhaps it would be better to start with his fiancée, Felicia Grant.

Then again, it would be a whole lot faster to go to Crenshaw. His office was just down the hall. If he didn't toss her out of it, he might have some very interesting things to say.

CHAPTER

Twelve

A*fter* several days of thinking that the gods must have it in for her, Amanda decided luck finally must be on her side. Jenny Lee was sitting at the desk outside Joel Crenshaw's office. If she had been there all morning, it just might save Amanda a direct confrontation with the publisher.

"Where's Marcia?" Amanda asked, hoping Joel's secretary hadn't simply made a quick trip to the copier.

"She had a dentist appointment. I'm subbing for her."

"Have you been here all morning?"

"Yes." Jenny Lee nodded toward the door and rolled her eyes. "Today of all days. He's been on a rampage ever since he got here. Apparently he knows all about last night's little escapade with the police. You should have heard him hollering at Oscar."

"I heard. Any idea how he found out? Somebody must have called him."

Jenny Lee handed Amanda a stack of messages. "Take

your pick. He hasn't even looked at them, though. He just stormed in here, told me to hold his calls, and slammed the door behind him. Didn't even say good morning. Not that I really care, mind you, but those little courtesies are important."

Amanda ignored Jenny Lee's dissertation on etiquette. "Then he knew before he got here. I wonder how," she said thoughtfully. "Check his calendar, would you? Any breakfast meetings?"

Jenny Lee regarded her curiously. "Why is this so important?"

"Because somebody's apparently worried enough about what I know to get Joel to call me off. It could be the same somebody who tried to kill me last night."

Jenny Lee turned pale. "I didn't even think about that."

"Well, I can't seem to forget it. My throat still hurts from trying to gasp for air and I've got black and blue marks on my arms. Now check the calendar for me."

"Sure," she said at once. She flipped over the pages of the red datebook on Marcia's desk. "Nothing."

Amanda stared at the page. His day was open until an eleven o'clock meeting. "Damn. I was hoping I could put this together without having to talk to him."

Jenny Lee immediately looked worried. "You're not actually thinking about going in there, are you?"

"I have to know who told him to pull me off the story."

"And you think he's going to tell you that? Amanda, the man is off the wall this morning. If he's like this after a workout, I can't imagine what his stress level would be without one."

Amanda's eyes lit up. "Workout?"

"Sure, he goes to Weights and Measures first thing every morning."

Amanda threw her arms around Jenny Lee. "That's it."

"What's it?"

"The connection. Now all I have to do is figure out who was at Weights and Measures this morning when he was there. Are Robert and Jackson usually there to open up?"

Jenny Lee seemed to be struggling to keep up. "I don't think so. I've been in a couple of times before work and it's usually one of the instructors who opens up."

"Which means it was probably another member who talked to him." She glanced at her watch. "Damn! It's nearly ten now. Unless I question the instructors, I'll never figure out who was there when they opened this morning."

"Sure you can. Just check the sign-in log. Sometimes at night they don't watch too closely because it gets so busy, but they're pretty strict about it in the morning."

"Jenny Lee, you are an angel. Will you do one more thing for me?"

Jenny Lee brightened at once. "Anything."

"Call Scott Cambridge and see if he knows the name of the spa in California where Carrie worked. If he does, call out there and see if you can find anyone who knew her."

"What should I ask, if I find somebody?"

"See if they know why she left," she said as Jenny Lee scribbled notes on her steno pad. "Maybe they'll remember if she really did follow some man to Atlanta. With luck, they might even recall his name."

"Got it."

"Thanks. I'm out of here. I'll check back with you later."

Just then Joel Crenshaw opened his office door. When he caught sight of Amanda, he glowered and opened his mouth for what she suspected was going to be a lengthy tirade. She waved and scooted into the elevator before he could get started.

Her only regret as she drove across town was that she would be incurring Donelli's wrath. He had warned her to stay away from Weights and Measures, but she didn't see any other way to check out her theory that Trace Weston had talked with Joel this morning between sit-ups.

Fortunately, she had her bag of gym clothes in the back of her car. They would have made a significant test case for any detergent on the market, but there was nothing she could do about that.

Toting the bag, she stopped at the reception desk to sign in. There were only a handful of names ahead of hers, so she flipped back a page and ran her finger down the list of members who had been in earlier. She found Joel's signature just a few lines down from the top, but Trace Weston's name wasn't there. She thought she recognized one of the other names—Franklin Gentry—but she couldn't recall where she'd seen or heard it. At the bottom of the page she came across another familiar name—Felicia Grant.

Now that was interesting. Was it possible that Felicia had been carrying messages for her fiancé? It didn't seem a likely role for her, but it was the only real lead she had.

After making sure that Felicia was no longer at the club, Amanda went to the pay phone in the locker room and checked the phone directory. Damn. The number was unlisted. That meant if she wanted to see Felicia she would have to go poking around in the membership files to find the address.

Ten minutes later she was dressed in her leotard, doing her stretching warm-ups in the vicinity of the office suite. The front office, Jackson's, was empty and dark. She could not see Robert's. Since that was where the membership files were kept, she would have to take her chances whenever the receptionist left her desk.

At the first opportunity, she darted into the suite and slipped quietly down the hall. The light in Robert's office was on, but she didn't hear any noise. She peeked around the doorway, mentally preparing an excuse for the visit if he turned out to be there. He wasn't. But there was a coffee cup on the desk and a letter in the typewriter. He apparently wouldn't be away for long.

At least this morning she didn't have to waste time searching. She went straight to the closet, opened the middle file, and rummaged through it for Felicia Grant's folder. She scribbled the address on Robert's memo pad and stuffed the paper in the top of her leotard.

She had just returned the file, when she heard Robert in the hallway giving instructions to the receptionist. Her heart slammed against her chest. She tried frantically to recall the excuse she'd dreamed up for being in his office, but her mind was too busy replaying the image of that towel being secured over her head. By the time she realized she could still breathe, she was on the verge of fainting.

"Oh, for God's sake," she heard Robert snap. "I'll fix the damn pipe myself. By the time we could get a plumber over here, the whole locker room would be under water. You just get the phone. If it's for me, take a message until I get back over here."

The receptionist muttered something, but Amanda couldn't hear the exact words. It sounded like something uncomplimentary about Robert's mother.

She took a deep breath and edged into the hallway. The receptionist's back was to her. She inched along the wall, hoping to make a run for safety. Her dash into the gym took her full speed into a very solid chest.

"Sorry," she murmured without looking up.

"Amanda?" She'd heard that voice when it was a warm caress. All things considered, she liked it better under those conditions. It was decidedly chilly now. In fact, outraged would just about describe the tone.

She gazed up into Donelli's disappointed, dark brown eyes. "Hi, there."

He clamped a hand around her elbow and propelled her through the health club so fast it could have qualified as jogging. She tried wrenching free of his grasp, but he was in no mood to surrender custody.

"Donelli, my things." As a delaying tactic, it was the best she could do.

"What about them?"

"I can't just leave them in the locker room."

He changed direction. "Get them. But if you're not back out here in exactly sixty seconds, I am coming in after you."

She glared up at him. "Has anyone pointed out to you what a bully you can be?"

"On my good days. Now move it."

Amanda briefly considered hiding out in the sauna, but decided it would be a wasted effort. Donelli in his present mood would have absolutely no qualms about storming into a roomful of half-naked women to retrieve her. She did, however, allow herself a full sixty-five seconds before going back to join him. She was not surprised to catch him with one foot already into the locker room.

To her irritation, she found there was something a little sexy about Donelli in a snit. She had a hunch there would be hundreds of opportunities for her to get to know this side of his personality, if they stayed together.

He didn't say another word until he'd marched her down the street and into the corner coffee shop.

"Coffee," he told the waitress, then looked at Amanda. "What about you?"

"As I see it, this isn't a social occasion."

"Whatever." When the puzzled waitress had gone, he rubbed his eyes wearily. "Okay, Amanda, explain."

"Explain what?"

"Don't you dare play dumb with me," he said furiously. "You know perfectly well what I'm talking about. I told you to stay away from Weights and Measures. Just in case you didn't want to take my word on the danger, there was that little incident last night in which you almost died. I thought that at least would get it through your thick skull that we are not dealing with some amateur. Carrie did not die accidentally. Whoever it was meant to kill her. It is entirely possible that that same person meant to kill you last night. If it's dumb for the criminal to return to the scene of the crime, it is incomprehensible to me that the would-be victim would show up for another round. Is any of this sinking in?"

"Not only do I understand, but I'm sure most of the people in here do."

Indeed, everyone in the place was staring at the two of them and had been ever since Donelli began talking about murder in decibels only slightly lower than those of a rock music station tuned to top volume.

"Then would you kindly try to make me understand. I love you, but your logic escapes me. Do you have a death wish? Are you so ambitious that you'll risk your neck for the sake of a headline? Do you do it just to torment me? What is it?"

"In the end, it's the same thing that drives you, Donelli. I want to know the truth. Now that may have started out as an objective, dispassionate search, but as you've just noted, I now have a personal stake in the answers."

He sighed. "I know you do, but so do I. Can't you trust me to find them for both of us?"

"It has nothing to do with trusting you. I can't just sit idly back and wait. It would drive me crazy. I was brought up to be independent, Donelli. I was also trained to look for answers. That's what an investigative journalist does. I can't turn into a simpering wallflower, just so you can play hero."

He winced and she swallowed hard. "Sorry. I didn't mean that the way it sounded. I know you're just worried about me, but, Donelli, I know how to follow up leads just as well as you do. You should know that by now. Can't we work on this together?''

He watched her intently for what seemed an eternity, then shook his head. ''I'm not going to talk you out of it, am I?''

She shrugged apologetically. ''Sorry. I know why you want me to stop, but I can't. Please, Joe, don't make me choose between my career and pleasing you.''

He mangled a straw before he finally spoke. ''Okay. You're right. We'll do it your way. What were you trying to find in there this morning?''

She explained about Joel Crenshaw's call to Oscar, his habit of working out at Weights and Measures before coming to work and finding Felicia Grant's name in the sign-in book.

''So what were you planning to do next?'' He groaned. ''Never mind. I can guess. You were going to see her.''

''She was a very nervous lady the last time I saw her. I figured it wouldn't take too much pressure to make her open up.''

''Do you have her address?''

She reached for the top of her leotard. He grinned and held up his hand. ''It'll wait until we get to the car.'' He took some money out and dropped it on the table. ''Okay. Let's go.''

''You're going with me?''

''I'm certainly not going to let you go over there alone and experience tells me I'm not going to stop you from going.''

This time when they stood up, Amanda tucked her arm through his and stood on tiptoe to give him an affectionate kiss. He deserved that and more for putting aside his fears for her out of deference to her need to know. "You're a very wonderful man."

Felicia Grant lived in a modest, two-story brick house in the Virginia-Highland area. Pink, yellow, and apricot roses bloomed in the small front yard. The only splash of red was a sporty Honda CRX at the front edge of a driveway that sloped sharply down to a shaded backyard. While the setting was pleasant, it was obvious that her engagement to Trace Weston was for Felicia Grant a step up the Atlanta social ladder.

"I don't suppose I could talk you into waiting in the car," Amanda said hopefully as Donelli stopped in front of the house. "She might speak more freely to me if I'm alone."

"Okay."

Amanda's mouth dropped open. "Just like that? Okay?"

He grinned. "Get going before I change my mind. I'll give you fifteen minutes."

"Donelli, I can't even get warmed up in fifteen minutes."

"Talk fast."

She decided she'd better take what she could get. When she rang the doorbell, she heard footsteps on the stairs inside, then a hesitation at the door.

"Who is it?"

"It's Amanda Roberts, Felicia. Could we talk for a minute?"

The door swung open. Felicia was dressed to go out in a blue linen suit with a flower on the lapel and a stunning sapphire solitaire in an antique gold setting at her throat. "I don't have a lot of time."

"No problem. I'll be quick."

Felicia peered over Amanda's shoulder. "Who's he?"

"A friend. He gave me a ride over. May I come in?"

"Of course. I'm sorry."

Amanda noted the antiques and expensive fabrics in the living room, the decorator touches that were important, rather than personal. It had been designed for show, not comfort. She perched on the edge of a stiff Victorian sofa. "Were you at the club this morning?"

"Yes."

"What time?"

A panicky expression clouded Felicia's eyes. She kept twisting her engagement ring around and around on her finger. "I got there about seven-thirty, why? Has something else happened?"

"I'm not sure. If you'll bear with me, I'll explain. Did you see Joel Crenshaw while you were there?"

"Who's he?" She looked absolutely nonplussed by the question.

"He's the publisher of *Inside Atlanta*. Your fiancé owns a sizable chunk of the magazine."

"Of course. Now I know who you mean. Trace has pointed him out to me a couple of times, but we've never met."

Amanda's spirits fell. "Then you didn't talk to him this morning?"

"No. If he's the man I'm thinking of, he said hello, but that was it. Why?"

"It's important for me to find out who Joel Crenshaw did talk to this morning. Did you see him with anyone else at the club?"

"I wasn't really paying any attention. I believe I saw him speak to a few people, but I don't think he spent any time with any one of them."

"Are you sure? What kind of mood was he in?"

"I don't know him well enough to judge his moods. I've merely seen him at a few of those mob scene social functions Trace has to attend."

"Did he seem angry or upset when you saw him?"

"Amanda, I'd like to help you, but I just don't remember."

Amanda sighed. "Okay. Thanks for trying. If you think of anything, you'll let me know?"

"Sure, but I still don't understand."

"Somebody put pressure on Crenshaw to get him to kill this story. I'm convinced it was somebody he saw at the club this morning."

"I see. I wish I could help."

They were at the door when Felicia put her hand out to stop Amanda. "Wait. I know who I saw him with. It wasn't until he was leaving, though. He ran into Franklin Gentry coming in. Franklin was quite agitated. He and this Mr. Crenshaw went into the snack bar. I didn't see them together again. Franklin came back into the gym a few minutes later."

"You know this Mr. Gentry?"

"Casually. I met him at some alumni fund-raiser for the University of Georgia. Trace introduced us."

Bingo.

"Thanks, Felicia. You've been a big help."

"Does this have something to do with what happened to Carrie?"

"I hope so. I'll be in touch."

As the front door closed behind her, Amanda glanced at her watch. She had twenty-two seconds to spare.

"Well," Donelli said when she got in the car. "Did you find out anything?"

"I found out that some guy named Gentry was with Joel at the club this morning. Felicia says she met him at a fund-raiser. Trace introduced them. My hunch is that it was Gentry who told Joel to kill the story and I'd be willing to bet that Trace Weston put him up to it."

Donelli shook his head. "Why wouldn't Weston just call Joel himself? We're not talking about some multimillion-dollar deal that requires discretion. If he wanted a story killed in a magazine he backs, he seems like the kind of man who'd give the order himself."

Amanda moaned. "I wish you hadn't said that."

"Why?"

"Because it makes too much sense." She hesitated. "Unless . . ."

"Unless what?"

"Unless he doesn't want his link to the story known."

"Maybe, but I'm still inclined to think this Gentry is the one we're after."

"Why would some university official care about a story about a health club?"

"Maybe he has a lifetime membership and wants to be sure the place doesn't close."

"Very funny. I'm serious, Donelli. If you're right, then we're missing something."

"Don't you have some university directories at the office? Let's go over there and see just what it is that Gentry does."

When they got off the elevator outside the magazine's offices, they could see Oscar pacing up and down through the newsroom. His tie was askew and his remaining hair was sticking out in every direction.

"There you are. Where the hell have you been? I've been beeping you for the last hour."

Amanda winced and pulled open the lap drawer of her desk, where her beeper was resting on top of some papers.

"A hell of a lot of good it's doing you there. What if there had been an emergency? Hell, there was an emergency."

Before Oscar could explain, Amanda's line rang. She grabbed up the phone. "Yes. This is Amanda Roberts."

"Amanda, it's Mack."

Her stomach flipped out of habit. But his voice did not have the power to affect her any more.

"What do you want, Mack? I'm very busy right now."

"You always were," he said wryly. "I won't keep you long, but there's something I think you ought to know."

"If you're calling to announce your engagement, Mack, don't bother. Your future plans no longer concern me."

"Amanda, will you lighten up and listen, please? I've heard some talk around campus about a reporter who's digging into something pretty explosive. Naturally, I thought of you."

"If that was meant to be funny, you missed the mark."

"No, actually I meant it as advice. If you are working on a story right now that has a university connection, be careful. Despite what you think, I do still care about you."

Amanda sighed deeply. She closed her eyes and rubbed her forehead, where she could already feel the first twinges of a headache. She bit back the first quick retort that popped into mind and said instead, "Okay, if you say so. Any details?"

"None. I'm sorry. Just a lot of talk about getting even with a reporter. This could have been idle boasting or it could have been deadly serious. Please, if you are involved, get yourself some protection."

"I'll think about it, Mack. I promise."

She hung up and sank down in her chair. She felt Donelli's hands begin to knead her shoulders, working at the knotted muscles that had formed during that very brief conversation. She wasn't sure whether it was hearing Mack's voice after all this time or the warning that had created the tension, but Donelli's touch felt very good. It reminded her of what was real and important in her life now. When this story was finished and in print, she and Donelli were going to spend time together and finally work things out.

"What did he want?" Donelli asked eventually. "Or would you rather not talk about it?"

"It's hardly personal. He was worried. He's heard some talk around campus that a reporter is digging into something pretty important, something that might affect the university. He doesn't have any details, but it fits with what we know about this guy, Franklin Gentry—he's a heavy hitter at the university."

She turned to Oscar. "Was Mack the emergency?"

"No, some other guy was calling every ten minutes looking for you. He said it was urgent and that you told him to call."

"Did he give his name?"

He looked at the pink message slip in his hand. "Scott Cambridge. Who the devil is he?"

Amanda grabbed the paper. "He was Carrie Owens's lover," she said as she dialed the number. He answered on the first ring. "Scott, this is Amanda Roberts."

"Thank God. Can you get over to my place right away?" He sounded very agitated.

"Are you okay? Has something happened?"

"Not exactly. I found out something today. I haven't told the police yet, because I can't quite figure out the connection, but I'm sure this is it."

"This is what?"

"The reason Carrie was killed."

CHAPTER
Thirteen

During the drive to the Wisteria Apartments, Amanda couldn't resist trying to guess what Scott had discovered. She ran through several scenarios until Donelli finally grew impatient. "Why don't you just wait until we get there and let him tell you?"

Amanda shot an equally impatient glance back at him. "It'll be more satisfying if I figure it out for myself."

"In that case, you can wait in the car this time and jot down your guesses. I'll let you know later, if any of them are right."

Since she had a feeling he might be serious, she grinned and suggested, "Go to hell, Donelli."

She was out of the car before he had even turned off the engine. But just when she would have burst through the entrance to Scott's building, she heard Donelli's footsteps pounding up the walk. He latched onto her arm and yanked her back. "Will you wait a minute?"

"Why? Afraid I'll beat you to the solution?"

"Damn it, Amanda," he growled in a low voice. "Don't act like a child. This is not a scavenger hunt. Hasn't it occurred to you that this could be a setup?"

She skidded to a halt. Her heart lurched unsteadily. "A setup?"

"Yes, as in walk through the door and get killed."

That was one scenario she hadn't thought of. It was definitely not her favorite. "Why . . . what . . ."

"Amanda, for all your instinctive trust in Scott Cambridge, you don't really know that he didn't kill Carrie himself. The heat has been turned up by several degrees in recent days. Maybe now he's decided he'd better get busy covering his tracks."

Even though she knew Donelli had to be wrong, she swallowed past a very large lump in her throat and stood back. "You first."

"Thank you."

Donelli led the way up the stairs and knocked on the door. It was opened immediately by a very frazzled Scott Cambridge. The usual self-confident smile had vanished. He was pale, his expression slightly dazed. He seemed even more shaken by the sight of Donelli.

"Who are you?"

"Joe Donelli. I came along with Amanda."

She peeked out from behind him and saw relief transform Scott's face. "Thank God. I haven't been able to sit still since I figured this out. If you hadn't shown up soon, I'd have gone nuts. I don't know what to do next."

"Take it easy," Amanda said, following him into the

apartment. She immediately noticed all the extra touches, the plants and pictures and knick-knacks that she suspected had been Carrie's contribution to the decor. A five-by-seven color photo of her was in one-half of a silver frame prominently displayed on an end table. A blow up of a snapshot taken of the two of them was in the other half. If Amanda had seen that look of mutual adoration in their eyes sooner, she would never have placed Scott on her list of suspects. When she caught Donelli staring at it, too, she shot him a smug look.

"What have you found out?" she asked Scott.

"I came across something last night. I tried calling you at the office, but I couldn't reach anyone and you're not listed in the Atlanta directory."

"I live outside the county," she said as she watched Scott lift a cushion on the sofa and remove several papers. Amanda would have found the secrecy amusing, if Scott hadn't been quite so nervous. He handed them to her as if he couldn't wait to get rid of them.

Intrigued by his demeanor, she studied the pages closely. They appeared to have been photocopied from a notebook. The pages were lined and one edge was jagged. Each page had a list of names. There were dates beside each name, along with a series of checkmarks. On the surface they seemed innocent enough, but obviously Scott saw something that escaped her. She gave them to Donelli, then waited as he looked them over.

"What are they?" she asked finally.

"It looks like a record of some sort of transactions," Donelli said.

"Possibly," she said. "But there's no mention of money."

"I know. That struck me as odd, too," Scott said.

Donelli looked closely at Scott. "I think we'd better start at the beginning. Where did you get these?"

"I found a notebook in Robert's office last night. It was after you all had left the club. He came in later to work out. One of the members had a question and he sent me into his office for a file. I got it and then I noticed the notebook on his desk. I just got a feeling about it, so I took a look. When I saw what it was, I copied some of the pages before I went back into the gym. I was afraid he'd come looking for me, so this is just a start. Every page in the notebook was filled with the same kind of stuff."

"Why would he leave this out on his desk, if it's so important?" Amanda asked. "Anyone could have come across it."

"No. He'd locked the office. Obviously he forgot that he left it out when he sent me back there."

"Do the entries make any sense to you?" Donelli asked.

Scott nodded. "I wish they didn't. I think Carrie must have stumbled across this, too."

Amanda moved closer to Donelli on the sofa and peered over his shoulder. "Are these members' names?"

Scott shook his head. "No, but I recognize most of them."

"Unfortunately, so do I," Donelli said. Amanda could tell he was beginning to make sense of Scott's discovery, while the implication continued to elude her.

"What's the connection to Weights and Measures, if they're not members?" Donelli asked.

"Most of them stop by occasionally," Scott said. He pointed to the most recent entry. "See this one? He was in the club last night right before I went into the office."

As she looked at the name, suddenly something clicked in Amanda's mind. "Isn't Kelvin Washington that football player Jenny Lee was carrying on about?"

"Yes," Donelli said.

"Where did you see him, Scott? Did he go into the snack bar?"

He stared at her blankly. "No. Why?"

"I've been following up on a hunch. I thought they might be using the snack bar as a front for drugs."

He shook his head. "It's not drugs. At least, not the kind you mean. These names, they're all local athletes. Some are professional, but most of them are from the colleges. There are even a few high-school football players."

Donelli shook his head. "Damn."

"What?" Amanda said.

"Steroids," Donelli said softly. "That's what you're thinking, isn't it, Scott?"

He nodded. "I'm almost certain."

Amanda stared at them. "Well, you two obviously know what you're talking about, but I still don't have a clue."

"Remember the Canadian runner who lost his gold medal in the Olympics? He'd been caught using steroids. There are rules against steroid use in most sports, but a lot of kids get into them when they're into bodybuilding."

"You mean kids who think they want to look like Mr. Universe or the Incredible Hulk?"

"Some of them just want to play football or some other sport," said Scott. "They don't seem to realize how dangerous steroids are. They've been connected to stunted growth with young kids and in adults they can cause impotence and liver disease. Even so, the number of teenage boys using them keeps going up."

"If Weights and Measures has been providing them illegally and Carrie found out about it, it would certainly be a motive for murder," said Donelli. "If word got out —and that's where you obviously fit in, Amanda—it would also be a hell of a scandal for the athletic programs at some of the schools."

"Just think of the millions of dollars generated by the college sports programs," Amanda said thoughtfully. Something else clicked. "So that could be how Franklin Gentry fits into this. Do you know him, Scott?"

"Sure," said Scott. "He's the athletic director at the University of Georgia. I'd forgotten about that. He's around all the time. He joined the club about the time Robert and Jackson bought it."

"Then he must have known about the steroids. Maybe he even had something to do with setting the club up as a distribution center. No wonder he wanted me to back off." Amanda felt that stirring of excitement in her blood that only happened when all the threads of a story were beginning to come together. "Okay, we have the motive."

"We *may* have the motive," Donelli corrected.

"Whatever. Who are the primary suspects now? Robert

and Jackson stay on the list. Personally I'd rule out Frank and Alana or do you think they could be distributing the steroids through the snack bar?''

''No.'' Donelli shook his head. ''You saw the kids hanging out in there. Remember, they looked more like junkies than bodybuilders. That's what made you suspicious in the first place.''

''I'm not crazy about Frank, but I agree,'' Scott said. ''If we were dealing with a drug ring, maybe, but this doesn't seem like something they'd be into. You have to really understand the college sports world to realize the potential market. Now they're banned in professional football, too.''

''Which brings us back to Franklin Gentry and Trace Weston. Gentry has ties to the university. Trace has ties there and to pro football,'' Amanda said, recalling a recent profile she'd seen of him. She looked at Donelli. ''What do we do next?''

''We talk to Detective Harrison,'' he said decisively.

She shook her head. ''He'll laugh us out of his office without better proof than this. Even you admitted we're still speculating.''

''Amanda, didn't you learn anything from last night's experience? If the police know what you're up to, they can offer at least some protection. They also might be able to make an arrest. As far as we know now, they have no idea about the steroid angle.''

Amanda wasn't wild about sharing her leads with the detective. But she didn't mind the idea of some police protection. And there was a certain benefit to getting Donelli more closely involved with the Atlanta police. She nodded her agreement. ''We'll go see Harrison.''

''Scott, you'd better come along with us,'' Donelli said. ''He's going to want your statement about the notebook. He'll need that before he can even think about getting a search warrant.''

Just as they closed the door to Scott's apartment behind them, Amanda's beeper sounded shrilly from inside her purse, where Oscar had pointedly placed it. She groaned impatiently. ''Damn. I'd better get it. Oscar's already thrown one tantrum today about my not staying in touch.''

She went back in and called the office. Jenny Lee answered. ''Thank goodness you checked in. Oscar's been having a fit.''

''Why?''

''You don't think he'd tell me, do you?'' Jenny Lee said in disgust. ''I'm just the lowly receptionist. Hang on a second and I'll get him.''

''Amanda, where are you?'' Oscar bellowed seconds later.

''With Scott Cambridge, why?''

''I just had a call from Larry. He was monitoring the police radio over at the *Gazette* and heard a call about an attempted suicide.''

Her heart thumped unsteadily. ''I assume this must have something to do with the story, since we don't do spot news.''

''You tell me what you think. The woman's name is Felicia Grant.''

* * *

Donelli made it to the hospital emergency room in what was for him record time. Even so, Amanda had only barely resisted the desire to reach across and put her own foot on the accelerator.

"That woman was not about to attempt suicide when I saw her this morning," she said for the dozenth time as they ran for the entrance, leaving Scott to park the car. The double doors whooshed open on a scene of chaos. There were people moaning and crying. Nurses were checking patients on stretchers, while others waited on plastic chairs to be called for treatment. In the typical crowd of patients with relatively minor injuries and distraught family members, she saw no sign of Felicia Grant or the police. Nor did she see Trace Weston.

Donelli went to the reception desk and asked the nurse about Felicia. The harried woman checked her log. "She's been moved upstairs. Take those elevators at the end of the hall."

"How is she?" Amanda asked.

"Lucky."

In the elevator, Donelli put his arms around Amanda and rested his chin on her head. She could feel the tension radiating from him. "This kind of stuff scares the hell out of me," he said. "This story is far from over and until it is, you're in just as much danger as Felicia."

A tingle of apprehension danced down her spine. "You think someone tried to murder her, too, don't you?"

"I'd say the odds are better than fifty-fifty." He tilted

her chin up, forcing her to meet his concerned gaze. "Promise me something."

"Another promise? What is it?"

"That you won't go chasing off by yourself again until the case is over. I know you get impatient, but there's not a story in the world that's worth dying for. If I can put farming on hold for a few days, you can do that much for me."

Instead of answering, she pulled his head down and brushed her lips across his. Donelli's reply was an urgent, possessive kiss that stole her breath and sent flaming color to her cheeks as the elevator doors opened.

Before they went to find Felicia Grant's room, Donelli took her hand. "I know what you were doing then," he said.

"Did it work?"

"It distracted me, Amanda. It didn't render me dumb. You're going to do whatever it takes to follow this story. Just promise you'll be careful."

"Always." She smiled. "I have a lot to live for, you know."

"Maybe that's something we should talk about," he said very, very softly. "Our future."

Amanda stared at him. He had never hinted at marriage before, never demanded anything more than their casual arrangement. Why now? Why today? Was it just the intensity and danger of the last few days that had put the idea into his head? Whatever it was, she had no idea how to respond and she feared her silence was hurting him.

But he grinned that crooked, confident smile that made

her heart pound. "I know," he said. "Now's not the time. But when this is over, we are going to talk about the future. Now let's go see what happened to Felicia."

He started briskly down the hall, with a dazed Amanda trailing along behind. It was several minutes before she realized that Detective Harrison was standing outside Felicia's room and that he and Donelli were speaking in hushed tones about what had happened. She struggled to focus on the present and not that elusive, risky future Donelli had been talking about.

"They're running tests now, but it looks like an overdose," the detective was saying.

"She was at home?" Donelli asked.

"No, she was at Weston's place. The housekeeper found her, when she went to the patio to call her to the phone."

"Who was the call from?" Amanda asked. At Donelli's puzzled look, she said, "I just wondered who knew where to find her."

He nodded approvingly. "Good question."

"Thank you very much."

"It was Weston on the phone, according to the housekeeper. He was calling to let her know their dinner plans or something. I haven't talked to him much. He's pretty shaken." His gaze came to rest on her. "I hear you spoke to her this morning."

Amanda scowled at Donelli, who'd obviously blabbed everything in his role as conscientious protector. "I went to see her, yes. She was in good spirits, certainly not a woman on the brink of committing suicide."

"Why did you go to see her?"

"Someone put pressure on my boss to pull me off this story. I thought she might be able to help me figure out who it was."

"And was she helpful?"

"Actually, she was. She told me she'd seen my publisher with a man from the university. It fit with some other information."

"Which I'm sure you plan to share with me," Detective Harrison said. "Let's go to the waiting room and have a talk."

Reluctantly, Amanda followed. Fully aware that Donelli would fill in any gaps she conveniently left in her story, she told the detective everything she knew, including what they now suspected about the steroids. To her amazement, he didn't laugh.

"It makes a hell of a lot more sense than drugs," he said, then asked a number of insightful questions and jotted down several things in his little leather-bound notebook.

"Let's get back to your visit with Felicia Grant for a minute. What time were you there?"

She looked to Donelli. "About eleven-thirty?" He nodded.

"What was her mood?"

"Overall I'd say it was pretty good. She seemed a little distracted and nervous when I arrived. She said she had to go somewhere."

"She didn't say where?"

"No."

Detective Harrison looked thoughtful. "That's odd."

"What is?"

"She had an appointment with a police psychologist for noon. That's obviously what she meant when she told you she had to be someplace."

"Was this for the hypnosis?"

His eyes widened. "She told you about that?"

"Not today. A few days ago. She was scared to do it. I even told her I'd come along, if she wanted me to."

"But she didn't mention it this morning?"

"No. Not a word. What happened? Did she go through the hypnosis?"

"No. She didn't show up."

"Has she told you why?"

"I haven't been able to talk to her yet. As soon as I can, you can bet it'll be the first thing I ask."

Amanda wasn't about to leave the hospital until she heard the answer to that question. She and Donelli found Scott downstairs, then went to the cafeteria for coffee. When the three of them wandered back upstairs, they were just in time to see the doctor coming out of Felicia's room. He stopped to talk to Detective Harrison.

"You can talk to her for ten minutes, no longer. The nurse is to stay in there and if at any time Ms. Grant seems too agitated, you will be asked to leave. Is that clear?"

The detective nodded.

"Could we go in, too?" Amanda asked, directing the question as much to Detective Harrison as to the doctor.

"It's okay with me, if the patient agrees," the doctor said.

"It might actually be helpful," Detective Harrison said. "If you've established some rapport with her, it might make her feel more comfortable."

The doctor went in to check. "She's agreed to have you all come in."

When they went into the large private suite, Amanda was shocked by Felicia's appearance. She looked pale and haggard and terrified. Trace Weston was sitting by the bed, clutching her hand tightly. He appeared to be in equally bad shape.

"Ms. Grant, I won't trouble you very long tonight, but there are a few questions I must have answered," Detective Harrison said in a surprisingly gentle tone.

Felicia nodded.

"Did you attempt to take your own life?"

Amanda was surprised by the bluntness of the question, but it didn't seem to upset Felicia. She shook her head adamantly. "Absolutely not. I've never had a prescription for any kind of tranquilizers. I don't even use aspirin, if I can help it."

"What about you, Mr. Weston?"

Weston appeared startled. "Me? I had some mild tranquilizers a couple of years back, but I don't think the prescription was still around."

"Then there were no tranquilizers in the house?"

"None that I knew of," Trace said.

"Ms. Grant, is it possible that you had too much to drink today, that you might not remember taking some medication?"

"Absolutely not. I've told you I avoid taking any medications and I don't usually drink during the day."

"Not even a little wine with lunch?"

"No. I never even had lunch. When I got to Trace's, I went out by the pool. There was a pitcher of lemonade there as always. I had some of that."

Detective Harrison picked up the phone, asked Trace for his number, and called the house. When one of the policemen on the scene got on the line, he told him to check for the lemonade.

"Send whatever's left and the pitcher to the lab." He hung up. "Did the housekeeper take the lemonade to the patio?"

"I don't know. I assumed she had, because it was there, but I didn't actually see her do it. In fact, I didn't even see her when I first arrived. I have my own key, so I just went in, changed, and went to the pool."

"Was there anyone else in the house as far as you know?"

"No one."

"The gardener's off today," Trace said. "There's no other help."

"No cars in the driveway when you arrived?"

Felicia shook her head.

"Who knew you were going to be there this afternoon?"

"The housekeeper, Trace . . . I guess that's it. I went over every afternoon, though. Any number of people knew that."

Detective Harrison frowned. "Okay, let's talk about earlier in the day. Ms. Roberts came to see you, right?"

"Yes."

"She says you were on your way out. Were you planning to keep your appointment at police headquarters then?"

Amanda was watching Trace Weston. She saw the look of puzzlement on his face, the tiny shadow that crossed his eyes. "Felicia, you didn't say anything to me about going to the police."

"I didn't want to upset you. I knew you didn't want me to go for the hypnosis."

Detective Harrison jumped on that. "Why didn't you want her to go, Mr. Weston?"

"Because she was already upset enough," Trace said defensively. "I didn't want her to go through any more."

"Was that what stopped you from keeping the appointment? Were you afraid of upsetting Mr. Weston?"

Felicia bit down so hard on her lower lip that Amanda was afraid she'd draw blood. "Felicia," she said softly. "Did something happen after I left?"

She nodded. Tears pooled in the corners of her eyes, then trickled down her cheeks.

"What happened?"

She stared helplessly at Trace before finally saying in a whisper, "I had a phone call."

"Who was it?" Detective Harrison asked.

"I'm not sure. It was a man, I think."

"Did he threaten you?"

"Not exactly," she said reluctantly.

"Please, Ms. Grant, this is important. You have to tell us what he said."

"He . . ." Her voice was choked and she clung to Trace's hand. "He said I'd be sorry if I went, that I wouldn't like what I remembered about Carrie's death."

"Did he explain what he meant by that?"

"Oh, God," she moaned softly. "I can't do this." She covered her face with her hands. Her shoulders shook with sobs. The nurse, who'd been watching silently, stepped forward, but Detective Harrison held out his hand to stop her.

"Ms. Grant, please."

Felicia turned to Trace, her eyes pleading for forgiveness. The appeal was so sad, so frightened that Amanda held her breath wondering what could possibly come next.

"He said . . . he said I'd remember seeing Trace in the steam room that night, that it was Trace who killed Carrie."

CHAPTER
Fourteen

Even Detective Harrison seemed thunderstruck. Amanda, though, felt curiously detached. She glanced at Donelli and saw that he, too, looked perplexed. Something didn't add up. She wasn't an especially big fan of Trace Weston's, but he didn't strike her as a murderer. He was too clean-cut, too Ivy League proper to suffocate a woman in a steam room. If Carrie Owens had posed a threat to him, he would have exacted his revenge in some other way.

She looked at him now. His eyes were wide with shock, his lips tightened in anger. There was no suggestion of guilt in his demeanor. In fact, he looked like a man trying extremely hard to control his temper. He had leapt to his feet upon hearing Felicia's revelation. He then paced up and down in the cramped space alongside Felicia's bed, stopping occasionally to slam his fist against the wall. He stared at Felicia, then shook his head and resumed pacing.

Everyone, including Detective Harrison, seemed to be

waiting to see what Trace would do next. When he finally spoke, his voice was laced with anger and just a hint of hurt and betrayal.

"You believed him, didn't you?" he said, his voice ragged. "Felicia, how could you possibly have believed that I would kill that woman?"

Felicia was crying even harder now. Again, the nurse stepped forward to intervene, but Felicia waved her away. "I didn't want to believe it," she said between sobs, "but I was so scared, Trace. You didn't want me to go to the psychiatrist. I thought maybe you didn't want me to remember."

"I didn't want you upset, damn it. That's all. I was just trying to protect you. I don't know what the hell you saw that night in the steam room. Maybe you didn't see anything. Even if you had, I thought you'd be safer if you didn't remember it. As long as the killer was convinced you had amnesia, I thought he wouldn't come after you. Obviously, I was wrong."

Felicia held out her arms. After a long, anguished hesitation, Trace sat down on the bed beside her. As they clung together, Felicia kept saying over and over, "I'm sorry, my darling. I'm so sorry."

Detective Harrison coughed subtly. "Mr. Weston, I think we'd better let your fiancée get some rest."

"But—" Trace began, but stopped when he saw the detective's intractable expression. He gave Felicia a final, reassuring kiss, then followed the rest of them from the room.

"I think you and I had better take a ride down to headquarters," Detective Harrison told Weston.

"You don't honestly think I had anything to do with Carrie Owens's murder, do you?"

"Let's just say I have to explore every possibility."

Trace nodded, his manner resigned. "I'll have my lawyer meet us there."

"I don't suppose—" Amanda began.

"Forget it," Detective Harrison said. "You've already had more access to this investigation than I'd like. From here on out, you'll wait for the releases and press conferences just like the rest of the media."

So much for gratitude and cooperation. She'd turned over all of her information and what did she get in return? A brush-off. She glared at Donelli and stalked off to find the car. Maybe by the time she found it, she'd feel less like strangling him. She doubted it, though.

She was leaning against the front bumper when Donelli finally caught up with her.

"Where's Scott?" she said.

"He went with Detective Harrison to give a statement about that notebook."

"Terrific! That's just great! They're off wrapping things up and we've been banished to the journalistic equivalent of Siberia."

Donelli chuckled. "That's not quite true, Amanda."

"What would you call it?"

"A challenge? An opportunity?"

"Bull—"

He held up a hand. "Enough, Amanda." He dangled the car keys in front of her. "I'll let you drive."

"Don't try pacifying me, you traitor. You could have pulled rank or something to get us into that interrogation room."

"Amanda, I don't hold any rank with the Atlanta police."

His extraordinary patience when she was being a royal pain only irritated her more. "And who's fault is that?" she snapped.

"Oh, for heaven's sake, get in the car. I'll drive."

She snatched the keys. "Not on your life."

She roared out of the parking lot. Donelli covered his eyes. She slowed down as they reached the traffic light on the corner and peeked over at him. Her heart had stopped thumping angrily and her blood pressure was dropping to a more normal range.

"Sorry," she apologized. "I just get so damned frustrated."

"I've noticed." He sounded far more understanding than he usually did after one of her outbursts. "Are you ready to calm down and listen for a minute?"

"Why not? I don't have anything better to do at the moment."

"That's too bad. I was hoping you'd be interested in catching the killer."

Her head snapped around. Horns blared behind her. "What do you mean?" she asked as she began driving again.

"You don't think there's enough evidence to charge Trace Weston any more than I do, do you?"

"No. Not really."

"Then while Detective Harrison is busy with him, it seems to me we should get down to some serious detecting."

"I assume you have an idea where to start."

"Let's just say I've been narrowing down the possibilities."

"And?" She was staring at him intently.

"Amanda, will you watch where you're going before we're both too incapacitated to investigate anything!"

She swerved back into the right lane. Donelli winced. She had a feeling this would be the last time he willingly allowed her behind the wheel.

"Go back to the office," he said. "If we arrive alive, we'll discuss this there."

"I'll keep my eyes on the road," she promised. "Just tell me what you're thinking."

"First, the motive for the murder appears to be the cover-up of that illegal steroid operation, right?"

"Right."

"Who stands to gain the most from keeping that quiet?"

"Robert and Jackson, I guess."

Donelli regarded her curiously. "Why do you put it that way?"

"Because they were going to sell the club to Trace Weston. Why would they do that, if they were using it as a front for this other business?"

Donelli shot an approving smile at her. "Very good, Amanda. So where does that leave us?"

She hesitated while she concentrated on pulling into her reserved space in the parking garage that served *Inside Atlanta*'s building. When she'd turned off the ignition, she turned to Donelli. "Maybe they weren't going to sell it. Or maybe they weren't as agreed on the idea as Robert told us. That would explain why Frank Marquez thought there was a possibility of expansion. Maybe one of them had been telling him that, while the other one was sneaking around trying to make a deal with Weston."

"Okay. Since we can't question Trace Weston right now, any ideas about whom we should talk to?"

"I vote for Franklin Gentry."

Donelli stared at her. "The twists your mind takes leave me breathless. Why on earth would you start with him?"

"Because he's our last unknown. If he knew about the steroids, then he's in with either Jackson or Robert or both."

"There might be an even closer starting point. What about Joel Crenshaw? Wouldn't you like to hear what he knows about Gentry? Gentry must have applied a lot of pressure to get him to call Oscar."

Amanda felt her stomach sink. If Joel Crenshaw had actually known the reason behind Gentry's request and had gone along with it anyway, it made him guilty of conspiracy in the steroid activities. She couldn't work for a man like that, which meant she would most likely have to leave Atlanta to find the kind of reporting job she wanted. She wondered if Donelli fully understood the implications of what he was suggesting. He was watching her now, his expression compassionate.

"Don't you think it's better to know?" he asked gently.

"But what if—"

He shook his head. "Don't. We'll cross that bridge when we come to it."

"Okay," she said reluctantly. "Let's do it."

When they got upstairs, Amanda decided that the meeting with Joel was one she'd have to handle alone. "I owe him the chance to explain without an audience."

"I suppose that's fair. I'll wait in Oscar's office. There are a couple of things I want to check out, too. We never did fully explore Carrie's life before she came to Atlanta. I'll make some calls."

"Check with Jenny Lee. She may already know something about that spa in California."

"She what?"

Amanda looked guilty. "I asked her to check for me."

"You have the shortest memory of any woman I've ever known."

"Just talk to her, Donelli. Save the lecture for later," she said as she started down the hall. "And stay out of Oscar's scotch."

Despite her desire to solve this case and write her story, her footsteps slowed as she neared Joel's office. She was not anxious to begin this confrontation. In fact, she'd been hoping to find Jenny Lee still sitting at his secretary's desk, but she had left. She was probably down in the newsroom this very minute revealing all sorts of new evidence to Donelli. She considered going back and joining them, but decided it would be cowardly. Finally, she drew in a deep breath and knocked.

"Yes?"

She opened the door and stuck her head in. "Got a minute?"

Joel put his pen down on his desk and stared at her. "After your deliberate defiance of my wishes, are you sure you want to come in here?"

She grinned. "Not really."

"Good, then come on in. I like a reporter who's not afraid to beard the lion in his den, even when she knows he's in a foul temper."

"I guess I was hoping your mood had improved," she said, taking the chair opposite him.

"I assume you're here to discuss the reason I told Oscar to pull you off that assignment."

She nodded. "More or less. Actually, I think I know the reason."

"Oh?"

"Franklin Gentry asked you to," she said bluntly and waited for his reaction. She had expected denial. She'd even allowed herself to hope for indignation or anger. Instead, Joel simply nodded.

"He did."

Amanda felt her temper flare. "And you just bowed down to his request? What kind of publisher does that make you? Damn it, Joel, I thought you wanted an aggressive, independent publication, one that wasn't afraid to take risks or step on the establishment's toes."

His face flushed. "I also wanted a responsible publication," he said quietly.

She was on her feet, leaning across the desk. "There is not a damn thing irresponsible about my reporting. You haven't even seen the story yet. You didn't ask about it. You based your decision on some outsider's influence. If you don't trust me, then I can't work here."

"You're jumping to conclusions," he pointed out, his voice suddenly cool. "If that's any indication of the way you do your reporting, then maybe you shouldn't be here."

Amanda swallowed hard and sat down, his words hanging in the air. Reluctantly, she conceded her guilt. "Okay. You're right. I did jump to conclusions. Why don't you tell me what Franklin Gentry said that convinced you the story shouldn't run."

"He told me that Trace Weston had ties to Weights and Measures, that he was negotiating a deal to purchase it. If you're as thorough as you say you are, then I'm sure you knew that."

Amanda nodded.

"He also reminded me that since Trace is a major backer of this magazine anything we wrote about the place could be perceived as a conflict of interest. If we puff it up as this great singles hangout, it stands to reason that business will boom and Trace will benefit. We're just getting established. I didn't want us to get accused of being a special-interest magazine right from the first issue."

Amanda stared at him in astonishment. "That's what he told you? He played on your integrity?"

Joel stared at her blankly. "Of course. What else could it have been? You've just confirmed that what he told me was the truth."

"A very carefully selected portion of the truth. He neglected to mention that Weights and Measures is apparently being used to distribute steroids to local athletes, including a few in his football program. He's the one with the financial stake, Joel. Forget Trace Weston. That was just a smokescreen. Franklin Gentry was trying to cover his own ass."

For a few seconds, Joel was incredulous. Then he became irate. At least he believed in Amanda's investigative skills. "That damned liar! Are you sure about this?"

"Sure enough that the police are investigating it now. We think that's why Carrie Owens was killed. She stumbled on the information and may have been threatening to release it."

"Dear God in heaven! Does Trace know?"

"He's being questioned right now. I'm sure that's one of the things Detective Harrison of the homicide division will be asking him." Relieved that Joel had merely been taken in and was not part of a conspiracy, she decided on a course of action. "How well do you know Franklin Gentry?"

Joel was still shaking his head in anger and disbelief. "We're in a lot of civic groups together. Outside of that I don't know him well, why?"

"Could you arrange a meeting with him? I'd like to confront him about this without him having time to prepare for it. I doubt if he killed Carrie himself, but I'd be willing to bet he could lead us to the person who did."

Joel appeared to give the idea serious thought. "I'm on a committee with him for an upcoming fund-raiser. I suppose I could call and tell him I need to see him about that. Where would you like to see him?"

"How about Weights and Measures?"

He cocked an eyebrow. "You really do like to live dangerously, don't you?"

"I prefer to think of it as having a flair for the dramatic."

As she waited for him to make the call, she wondered if Donelli would see it that way. Probably not, she decided, just as Joel nodded.

"Thanks, Franklin. I'll see you there in an hour then."

When Amanda started from the office, Joel was right on her heels. "Oh, no, you don't. This is one interview your publisher intends to sit in on."

She decided there might be a certain psychological advantage to appearing as a united front.

"Okay. Let me talk to Donelli and we'll get going."

The meeting in Oscar's office lasted less than five minutes. Everyone was astonishingly agreeable for a change. Even Donelli made only a token protest, which he quickly withdrew when she explained the role she had in mind for him.

"With Franklin Gentry's unwitting cooperation, we're going to bait a trap. It'll be interesting to see who bites."

"You already think you know who it's going to be, don't you?" Donelli said.

"I have my suspicions," she said with coy reticence.

"I think you'd better share them with the rest of us," Donelli said. "We won't be able to do a hell of a lot to protect you otherwise."

"If I tell you and I'm wrong, you'll be watching in the wrong direction. I think this way is better."

Donelli grinned at her. "Very wise."

She grinned back. "And just when you thought I was totally impetuous."

"This is the sort of surprise twist in your personality I can live with."

"I'll keep that in mind."

"If you two are through expressing your mutual admiration, don't you think you ought to get out of here?" Oscar grumbled.

"Don't be grouchy just because we're leaving you behind," Amanda said, dropping a kiss on his forehead.

Oscar blushed to the roots of his remaining hair. "Go. Be careful."

In the doorway Amanda turned back. "If you're planning to call Detective Harrison, wait an hour or so, would you? I'd hate to have him interrupt this little scenario and spoil the ending."

Donelli chuckled. Oscar looked so guilty she knew that was exactly what he had in mind. "Will you go before you miss the damned deadline and I have to fill the magazine with wire copy," he snapped. "We're not putting out an annual report, you know."

CHAPTER
Fifteen

W*hen* Amanda, Donelli, and Joel arrived back at Weights and Measures, she suggested the two men stake out the gym, while she detoured for a quick talk with Frank Marquez. She silenced Donelli's protest with a kiss. It was turning into a habit.

In the snack bar Marquez greeted her arrival with suspicion and open hostility. Apparently Alana had filled him in on her visitors the previous night.

"You are crazy," he shouted. *"Muy loca, comprende?"*

"I made a mistake," Amanda admitted, glad there was no one around to witness the outburst. "But I'm sure you can understand why we jumped to that conclusion. If you want to help me find the real killer, you'll stop yelling and talk to me."

His gaze narrowed. "Why should I want to help you with anything? You accuse me of having an affair with Carrie. You discuss this with my wife. You accuse her of murder. Now you want my help? Why? Why would I help you?"

"Because Carrie was your friend," she said softly.

His tense shoulders slowly relaxed and she noted the first evidence of genuine sadness in his dark eyes. "*Sí*," he said. "She was my friend, but she, too, was *muy loca*."

"Then help me. Tell me exactly what she knew that put her in so much danger."

When he continued to hesitate, she asked, "Was it about the steroids being sold out of the club?"

"*Sí*," he admitted finally.

"Had someone been threatening her?"

"*Sí*. She was very much afraid. She wanted to go, to leave here, you know, but she couldn't. She needed money and she could not get it."

"Who was threatening her?"

"Of that I am not sure. She would not say. It could have been Roberto or Jackson, but maybe not."

"You said the other day that Robert and Jackson were thinking about expanding and opening a second fitness club. Did they actually tell you that?"

"*Sí*. Roberto told me. Then I heard rumors there would be a sale. He would not tell me if that was true."

"Did you ever ask Jackson?"

"No."

"Thanks, Frank."

"This has been a help?"

"Yes," she said, responding to the sadness she saw in his eyes. "I think tonight the police may be able to catch Carrie's killer."

Convinced that she knew the identity of the killer, Amanda went back into the locker room to change.

By the time Franklin Gentry arrived at Weights and Measures, Amanda had arranged what she considered to be the perfect setup for baiting a trap. Donelli was working out on one of the weight machines. She was back on the exercise bike trying to pace herself. Joel was on the bike next to hers, pedaling about ten miles an hour faster and not even breathing hard. She glared at him, then turned her attention to Gentry.

As the athletic director crossed the room toward Joel, his expression was jovial enough, but as he spotted Amanda he hesitated.

"What's she doing here?" he asked in a tone that would not have qualified him as a welcome-wagon volunteer.

"She's still working on that story we were talking about the other day," Joel responded cheerfully. He was obviously enjoying his role. "A few more interviews and she'll have everything she needs. I have to thank you for piquing my interest in that feature."

Franklin Gentry looked as though he might faint. He turned pale. He grabbed a handkerchief from his pocket and wiped his suddenly damp forehead. "I thought you were going to drop that story because of the conflict of interest."

"Well, I got to thinking about that and decided it might not be quite as bad as you'd indicated. I mean Trace hasn't bought this place yet. The story could run in the next issue, before the deal's even closed. In fact, once he knows all the facts, he may decide to drop his bid for the club."

Doubt flickered in Franklin Gentry's pale blue eyes. Obviously he couldn't figure out whether to protest or let well enough alone. "So," he said finally. "What's your angle? Is it that singles approach I've heard everyone talking about?"

"It started out that way, but now I think we're onto something much better, something with a solid news angle," Amanda said. "I wouldn't be surprised to see us win a major award with this one."

Gentry swallowed hard. "You mean you're going to exploit that poor girl's unfortunate death?"

"I wouldn't call it exploitation. I think a better approach would be to explore the reason behind her death. I don't suppose you have any theories about that, do you, Mr. Gentry?"

He swiped at his brow again. "Me? No. Why would you ask? I didn't even know her."

"But you are a member here, aren't you?"

"Yes. I mean I didn't know her well. Maybe she just got mixed up with the wrong crowd. She was single, wasn't she? Maybe she picked up the wrong guy."

"That's certainly one possibility," Amanda conceded. Gentry looked relieved. "Except for the fact that she was living with someone with whom she was very much in love. Scott Cambridge. You must know him. He's an instructor here."

"Sure. I think I know which one he is." He glanced at Joel, then toward the front door, his expression desperate. "I thought you wanted to meet with me about the fund-raiser."

"In a minute, Franklin. I think Amanda may have a few more questions."

Amanda smiled. "Just one, actually. Do you mind?"

The friendly tone seemed to calm him. "Okay, sure. What is it?"

"What was your cut of the steroid operation?"

A visible tremor swept through Franklin Gentry, and Amanda thought for a minute he was going to keel over right at her feet. For an athletic man, he didn't hold up particularly well under pressure. Still, with admirable bravado, he tried to tough it out. "I'm afraid I haven't the slightest idea what you're talking about."

"Oh, really? You do know Kelvin Washington, don't you? I talked to him just a few minutes ago. He had some very interesting things to say about you." It was pure bluff, but Amanda hoped it was close enough to the mark to terrify him. She watched and waited.

Gentry braced himself against a weight machine. He'd given up mopping his brow and sweat trickled down his cheeks. "He's a kid. You certainly aren't going to take his word over mine, are you?"

"In this case, it seems like he'd have very little reason to lie. He said he'd talked to you about needing to put on a little bulk before the season started and you sent him right over here. I was here myself the night he came to check the place out."

"So, what's the big deal? I sent him here because this place has good instructors and good equipment. You'll never prove it was anything more than that."

"It's odd, then, that there's no record of him signing up for a membership, don't you think?"

"Maybe he hasn't made up his mind yet."

"Or maybe he found a quicker way to achieve the same end. Thanks for your time, Mr. Gentry. You've been a huge help," Amanda said softly, getting off the bike.

She walked away, leaving him with Joel.

"Damn you, you can't let her do this!" he was shouting as she went toward the locker room. She watched as he stomped off and went straight to the pay phones.

Five minutes later, wrapped in a towel, Amanda was in the steam room. She had the place to herself. She had seen to that earlier by putting an "out of service" sign on the door. If she was right, it wouldn't stop the killer from looking for her in here, but it would keep out other unsuspecting members.

Her pulse was racing unsteadily as she waited, her eyes on the door. Only a dim light visible through the thick, stifling steam told her where it was. The hot air seared her lungs. Perspiration trickled between her shoulder blades, then formed on her forehead and chest. Finally the door swung open, letting in a tantalizing whiff of cool air.

Suddenly the scant light in the steam room clicked off, ending what little visibility had existed. Amanda's heart began to pound like a jackhammer as a dark shape moved toward her.

"You had to push it, didn't you, Amanda?"

The voice surprised her. She thought she'd calculated all the possibilities, but this had been the one with the longest odds.

"You couldn't just do your little feature story and let it go. You're a damned good reporter, better than I thought."

"Thanks for the compliment, Mr. Weston," she said, astonished that there was no tremor in her voice, no hint of her surprise. "You're not so bad yourself. You had us all fooled in your fiancée's room tonight. That was quite a performance. Felicia's going to be devastated to learn the truth."

"Performance?" He paused. "Every word I said in there earlier was the truth. I didn't kill Carrie Owens."

Amanda's pulse seemed to skid to a stop. "You didn't? Then why are you here?"

"Because you're interfering and I thought I'd better warn you, just as I did her. This is a dangerous game, Amanda. The stakes are very high. Get away while you still can."

With her head reeling as she tried to sort through all the angles, Amanda felt her knees go weak. She sank down on the lowest tile bench. It didn't help that she was suddenly very much aware that she was sitting there in a towel, while Trace Weston was fully clothed. For that fleeting instant when she'd thought he was the killer, it hadn't seemed to matter. Now it seemed to put her at a distinct disadvantage.

"How did you get away from the police station so quickly?"

"Actually, I have you to thank for that. When your boss called Detective Harrison to tell him what you were up to, he released me until tomorrow."

"Were you in here the night Carrie was killed? Did Felicia see you leaving the steam room?"

"Yes. I took a chance coming back here. I wanted to warn Carrie the same way I'm warning you that this has gotten out of my control, that I could no longer protect her. When I got here, she was already dead."

"Why did you want to protect her? I don't understand."

"Save us both some time. What exactly do you think you know, Amanda?"

She knew, for one thing, that she was about to melt into a puddle on the floor of this steam room, but she supposed that wasn't what he meant. "I know about the steroids. You are involved somehow with that, aren't you?"

He sighed heavily. "No. Oh, I knew about it all right. Carrie told me. She and I had known each other before."

"In California," Amanda said with sudden certainty.

He chuckled. "Right again. You really are thorough. Yes, we'd met when I spent a week at a spa out there. She came to Atlanta shortly after that and we had a brief fling. I got her a job here. Then she found out about this damned steroid thing. She told me about it. She realized she was in danger and she wanted enough money so that she and Scott could get away. I told her I'd give it to her, but I wanted more time. I wanted to get enough evidence to be able to put a stop to it. I told her I'd protect her as long as she stayed here and fed me information." He lowered his head. "God, I failed miserably at that, didn't I?"

"Why didn't you just go to the authorities from the beginning?"

"I suppose because I wanted to try to minimize the damage to the university. When you attain a certain amount of power, you begin to think you can control the world. I'm a big supporter of that school. I thought I could buy the club and clean it up, end the operation or at least send it somewhere else. It would have worked, too. Jackson wanted to sell the place to me."

"I knew it," Amanda said. "He was behind it."

"Behind the steroids? No. I don't think he even knew about them until recently. He found out when Robert refused to sell. Things were going so well, Robert wanted to expand, open another club. He got greedy."

"Then who killed Carrie?" Amanda said, just as the door to the steam room whispered open again.

"I did," said Robert Barnes, as he stepped into the foggy shadows.

Through the suffocating steam, Amanda saw the gun in Robert's hand. It was pointed right at her chest.

"It's too late, Robert," Weston said calmly. He was either fearless or foolish. Amanda decided not to debate which. "The police will be in here any minute. It's a trap."

"They won't catch me in it," he boasted. "I'll have a hostage." He touched Amanda's chin with the tip of the gun. "Your boyfriend wouldn't want anything to happen to you, would he?"

Amanda was glad she was sitting down, because she wasn't at all sure how much longer she could have remained standing. With the blood pounding in her ears, she nearly missed the soft click outside the steam room. She kept her eyes glued to the glass doorway behind Robert.

There was no point in looking at the gun. She knew exactly where it was.

Weston began to talk, softly, insistently. "Robert, give it up. You don't want to kill anyone else."

"Why not? They can only put you in prison for life once. You know, I don't understand you, Weston. How did you make all that money? You could have had a piece of this action and you turned it down. We could have franchised it and been billionaires."

"After you earn the first few million, it's only force of habit that keeps you going," Weston said. "I already have more money than I could possibly spend in this lifetime. I didn't need to earn more by messing up the health of a bunch of kids who didn't know any better."

Slowly, the room was clearing. Amanda kept her eyes focused just beyond Robert. She slid her hand across the tile and touched Weston's hand. Only the slight movement of his fingers told her he knew what was happening. She took a deep breath and gave an almost imperceptible nod. Then, on the count of three, she dove to the side. Weston went the other way as a shot splintered the glass door and went into Robert's shoulder, sending his gun clattering uselessly to the floor. He knelt, clutching his shoulder and grimacing up at the door.

Amanda stayed huddled right where she was until the door opened and Donelli came in, followed by Detective Harrison. Donelli stepped gingerly through the glass and pulled her up and into his arms.

"Did you get it all?" she asked, a quiver in her voice.

"Every bit," the detective said.

Weston stared at her in astonishment. "You had the room bugged?"

"I may be impetuous, Mr. Weston, but I'm not stupid. I wasn't about to let this thing fall apart for lack of a confession."

"Where exactly is the bug?" he said, regarding her with blatant interest.

"Inside the towel. Where else?"

He laughed. "If you tell me you have a bulletproof vest on under there as well, I might have to demand to see it."

"In that case, I'll never tell," she said.

Detective Harrison was shaking his head. "I suppose I should thank you, Ms. Roberts, but a part of me would like to throw you in jail for disobeying my orders."

She grinned at him from the safe circle of Donelli's arms. "Which part's winning?"

After a full minute, he finally said with obvious reluctance, "Thanks. You have a lot of nerve. You, too, Donelli. Any time you want to get into police work, let me know."

"See, Donelli, what did I tell you?" Amanda gloated.

Detective Harrison laughed. "I meant both of you."

When they had handcuffed Robert and helped him out, Donelli tightened his arms around Amanda. "I suppose it would be terribly indiscreet if I took advantage of your present state of undress."

"Terribly," Amanda concurred.

"Just one kiss, then. To be sure you really are okay."

"Of course, but just one."

When one had turned into two and two had become

three, there was a pounding on the door. Joel poked his head in. "If you two don't get out of there, Oscar's going to come in after you. He wants to make sure his star reporter is in one piece."

Donelli gave a throaty chuckle. "Tell him I can vouch for it."

"You know Oscar," Amanda said. "That'll never be good enough. It's only hearsay."

Donelli groaned. "Okay, Amanda. Let's head for the showers."

"Separately, Donelli," she said, when she caught a new gleam in his eyes.

"Oh, hell."

"Yes," she said in heartfelt agreement.

EPILOGUE

Donelli's mouth was moving, but no sound was coming out.

"What did you say?" Amanda shouted.

He reached over and removed the earplugs she'd put in. "Amanda, I thought you told me you could shoot a gun," he said, staring pointedly at the target downrange.

"I can," she said indignantly. "There's a hole right where the bullet went through. Do you need glasses or something?"

"Amanda, the hole is in his toe."

"So? You didn't say I was supposed to kill the guy. I wounded him. He can't run after me with his toe shot off."

He groaned. "I suppose there is a horrible sort of logic in that. Should I assume that you could hit something more vital if you really tried?"

"I can't speak for you, but I'm a reporter, Donelli. We never assume anything."

"Then aim for the guy's heart this time."

She replaced the earplugs, then fired off the remaining rounds in quick succession. They hit the target with complete accuracy. Even she was impressed.

It had been nearly two years since she'd fired a gun. The New York police had seen to it that she knew how when she'd been in the middle of investigating a judicial corruption scandal. They'd suggested it right after the car bomb went off. At that stage, she'd have taken up a bow and arrow if they'd recommended it.

Even though she could shoot well, it didn't mean she liked guns or what they represented. As soon as she could, she returned the weapon to Donelli. "Satisfied?"

He nodded his approval. "That'll do. I want you to keep the gun."

"No."

"Amanda, it won't help you if you don't have it."

"I don't want it. If I need protection, I'd rather have you."

"That is not a liberated attitude."

"I can live with it."

He regarded her with a faint smile. "Can you really? Does that mean you'll move in with me?"

She reached up and touched his cheek. "Not yet, Donelli."

"Why not? You love me. I love you. What's it going to take? An act of God?"

"Just time. We still have things we need to work out."

"Such as?"

"Are you going to think about Detective Harrison's offer?"

"Are you?" he retorted.

"Of course not. I am perfectly happy as a reporter."

"And I am perfectly happy as a farmer, or I would be if I could spend more time doing it instead of chasing around the state protecting your backside. Do you have any idea how many weeds can grow when you turn your back for a few days? They've taken over the damned garden."

She stared deep into his eyes. They were contented, sparked by very real indignation over the audacity of those blasted weeds. There wasn't a shadow of a doubt in his eyes or his tone. "You really like spending your days digging in all that dirt?" she said, her voice still doubtful.

"It's a little more complicated than that, but yes." He regarded her speculatively. "Maybe if you stuck around for a couple of days, you'd understand it better."

"Donelli, I am not going to pick your tomatoes for you."

"What about the lettuce?"

"Forget it."

"Maybe you'd like to ride on the tractor then?"

"Why in God's name would I want to do that?"

"Consider it research. You wouldn't write a story without investigating all the angles, would you?"

"Is that a trick question?"

He ignored the jibe. "Then how can you make judgments about farming, when you haven't even tried it?"

"You're not going to be happy until I've got dirt under my fingernails and on my nose, are you?"

"I don't think you'll be happy until you accept my lifestyle. This seems like one way to get you to do it. Consider it a payback."

"For what?"

"For my chasing around after murderers for you without complaining."

"Without complaining?"

"Okay, with only a modest amount of complaining."

"I'm not sure I'm crazy about the deal."

"It's the only one you're getting. Think about the benefits of my farming."

"Which are?"

"You get all those fresh vegetables."

"I don't mind shopping the farmer's market."

"I only work days."

"You go out there at dawn. That's sick."

"I am available whenever you need a little professional advice from a trained detective."

"I'm sure Detective Harrison would consult with me, now that he respects my journalistic skills."

"In bed, while he massages your tired feet?"

She grinned. "He might be willing to work on that."

Donelli scowled. "Let's go, Amanda."

"Where?"

"Home."

"Why?"

"Are you planning to go through all those journalistic questions . . . who, what, where, when, why . . ."

"Not if you'd give me a straight answer."

"I thought we'd spend the rest of the afternoon . . . consulting." He slid an arm around her waist and dusted kisses down her neck until her breathing became uneven.

"Donelli?"

"Hmm?"

"How much do you know about cat burglars?"

He went very still. "Cat burglars? Why would you ask a thing like that?"

"I'm consulting."

"Can't you even wait until the ink is dry on this last story?"

"You know what they say about idle hands."

"I can think of better ways to occupy your hands." He kissed each finger—slow, lingering kisses—all the while keeping his gaze locked with hers. When he drew one finger deep into his mouth, she felt as though she were melting inside. "What did you want to know about cat burglars?" he said as he guided her hands down to the front of his jeans.

"Hmm?" she responded vaguely as she felt his body come alive to her touch.

"Let's go home, Amanda."

Home. His? Hers? Either way, it was definitely more interesting than cat burglars.

For now.

ROBERTS AND DONELLI ARE BACK ON THE CASE...

IN FOUR DELIGHTFUL MYSTERIES!

"A pair of sleuths that are believable, appealing, and immensely entertaining."
—*Mystery News*

☐ **HIDE AND SEEK**
(B36-405, $4.99 USA) ($5.99 Can.)

☐ **TIES THAT BIND**
(B36-117, $4.99 USA) ($5.99 Can.)

☐ **BANK ON IT**
(B36-454, $4.99 USA) ($5.99 Can.)

☐ **RECKLESS**
(B36-549, $4.99 USA) ($5.99 Can.)

Warner Books P.O. Box 690
New York, NY 10019

Please send me the books I have checked. I enclose a check or money order (not cash), plus 95¢ per order and 95¢ per copy to cover postage and handling,* or bill my ☐ American Express ☐ VISA ☐ MasterCard. (Allow 4-6 weeks for delivery.)

___Please send me your free mail order catalog. (If ordering only the catalog, include a large self-addressed, stamped envelope.)

Card # ______________________________

Signature ______________________ Exp. Date ________

Name ______________________________

Address ______________________________

City ______________ State ________ Zip ________

*New York and California residents add applicable sales tax. 549